EXPATS

To Dorothy —
a friend and fellow
lover of Spain

[signature]
08. XI. 07

EXPATS

Four seasons in *Spain*

A Novel

GERALD HOUGH

iUniverse, Inc.
New York Lincoln Shanghai

EXPATS

Four seasons in Spain

Copyright © 2007 by Gerald J. Hough

iUniverse books may be ordered through booksellers or by contacting:

iUniverse
2021 Pine Lake Road, Suite 100
Lincoln, NE 68512
www.iuniverse.com
1-800-Authors (1-800-288-4677)

This is a work of fiction. Other than the public figures and the credit card company American Express, all of the characters, names, incidents, organizations, and dialogue in this novel are either the products of the author's imagination or are used fictitiously.

ISBN: 978-0-595-43351-3 (pbk)
ISBN: 978-0-595-87677-8 (ebk)

Printed in the United States of America

Para Margarita,

siempre

There are approximately four million Americans living overseas.

U.S. State Department

—I've often wondered why you don't go back to America. Did you abscond with the church funds? Did you run away with a senator's wife? I'd like to think that you killed a man. It's the romantic in me.
—It was a combination of all three.

Casablanca

—You know, nobody here is <u>from</u> here.

Overheard in a bar

SUMMER

Chapter One

A fresh bouquet of fireworks bloomed in the evening sky as the band lit into *Seventy-Six Trombones*. I looked down the sloping lawn of the embassy at the crowd outside the gates. I wondered what they thought when they saw the richest people on the planet celebrate their big day with a straw boater, a bow tie and a hot dog. An old couple peered through the fence. He was dark and ferret-like with a rolled-up newspaper under his arm. She was lumpy and pinched under a brown kerchief. They could have been Albanian. Around me, though, people looked pink and white. And some did wear boaters.

Along the fence, U.S. Marines patrolled the perimeter. A week earlier, the U.S. Military attaché had been assassinated, along with his driver. Claiming responsibility was an anti-American group demanding withdrawal of all U.S. troops from Spain. Since then, I no longer got the *Herald Tribune* at newsstands and I tried not to speak English in public. The embassy had even posted a notice suggesting Americans refrain from wearing baseball caps, oxford-cloth shirts, khaki pants and moccasins, which pretty much summed up my wardrobe.

A new burst of fireworks creamed magenta against the deep blue sky, and I got a sharp whiff of gunpowder. With the warm air and the hot dogs and the beer, I felt an urge to go to a baseball game. Why didn't they play baseball in Spain? The earth was infield-red, the people were boisterous and used to heartbreak. Why not? Six months after leaving New York, I'd discovered how selective nostalgia was. I didn't miss Madison Avenue, or even my old apartment in the Village. But I did miss Yankee Stadium.

Randy Blanchard arrived with a tray of hors d'oeuvres—deviled ham, Philadelphia Cream Cheese and chives, and cucumber sandwiches, no crust. Did food this WASP still exist in the States?

The embassy gave a yearly Fourth of July party and invited Americans living in Madrid to mingle with the staff. Invitations were coveted despite the nonchalance feigned by those who got them. Randy was on the list because his mother had been to Emma Willard with the ambassador's wife. The latter now waved brightly at us. She was a tanned, slim woman in a very green skirt. Her husband was huge, with cottony hair, and looked affable and rich. He must have been a good fullback sixty or seventy pounds earlier. I went to get a Budweiser.

—They have <u>Budweiser</u>?—Randy couldn't believe it.

—And Jack Daniel's and Southern Comfort. You can probably get Skippy Peanut Butter.

A woman came up from behind and covered my eyes.

—Guess who?

—From your perfume, I'll say ... Eleanor Roosevelt.

Petria Holvin laughed.

—Kevin! Don't you know Diorissimo is compulsory at these things, like espadrilles? By the way, you guys still going to Pamplona?

San Fermín was only three days away and we had vaguely talked of going.

—Not only am I going,—announced Cottie Chubb—I have a room at Los Reyes and ringside seats.

—Are you going to run?—Asked Petria with hushed awe.

—Absolutely—declared Cottie.

—And I'm going just to document <u>that</u>—said Randy.

I couldn't take off from work to go to Pamplona. Besides, I was too enamored of Hemingway's account to go see what today's *fiesta* had become—a Spanish edition of *Guys Gone Wild*.

—Whoa. Nine-thirty. I'm meeting Mar for dinner in an hour.

—Randy! You mean you didn't bring her?—Exclaimed Petria.

—Nope. She still thinks Americans are tasteful and suave.

—How could she possibly still think that?—Shot back Cottie.

Randy paused, then blurted:

—Oh, touché, Mr. Chubb.

Cottie was an odd transplant. He spoke no Spanish, had no job in Spain and didn't appear to be looking for one. We'd both worked on the literary magazine at Lawrenceville and I wondered whether he was a closet novelist; and what he lived on. Though he could beadily dispute the tab at a Chinese restaurant, he had handmade suits. That year he had tickets to Wimbledon.

We decided to have dinner at a *tapas* bar called Bocaíto.

—Yeah! Joel is on tonight. We can try to mix him up; play 'stump the *tapas* chef'—said Randy.

It was after ten when we left the embassy. But the sky still held that purple light that so lingers in Spain. Out on the street, the crowds were gone. But the big armored cars of the *Guardia Civil* were still there, up on the sidewalk. There to protect us.

From Cottie Chubb's viewpoint, it wasn't so much that he'd run with the bulls in Pamplona, but that the bulls had run with <u>him</u>.

—Had 'em all the way. Sprinted into the ring ahead of the pack.

—Well, you did <u>start</u> quite a ways up the street—murmured Randy, squinting at his sherry.

Cottie jumped out of the leather armchair.

—Well, yes! Who starts at the bottom with the Aussies and the Krauts, who've been up all night and can barely stand? They're the <u>real</u> danger, Mister. I don't care how much sawdust they throw on that street—the muck from the drunks is an unacceptable hazard.

Mar came into the living room with a platter of cured ham and olives.

—Cottie, have yew gaw-ten the pictures back?

Her English was crisp and faintly British.

—No, but I dropped them off to be developed.

—Way to go, Cottie. Did some heavy lifting there—said Randy.

—Well, <u>you</u> pick up three rolls of film at 500 *pesetas* a pop.

—Why? I <u>took</u> the pictures. You are <u>in</u> the pictures.

It was Saturday. We were in the apartment that Mar and her sister Verónica had on Plaza de Santa Ana. It had wooden floors, lacquered like old violins. Three large bedrooms, one converted into a studio for Mar's painting, were off a long central hallway that led to a kitchen as large and white as an operating theater. The ceilings were twelve feet high and two ornate balconies overlooked the plaza.

The doorbell rang and Mar let in Joel Marx. They kissed on both cheeks.

—Here: mushroom caps from the restaurant. I stuffed them with crab-meat, *gruyere* and garlic. Go slide them in the broiler, eight minutes—to die for. So, where're we going for lunch?

Joel Marx was the unlikeliest chef I'd ever met: a short, wiry Bronx kid who went to Fordham on a wrestling scholarship, to Culinary Institute of America after that, and did two years as pantry slave at the Waldorf. He'd come to Madrid with no Spanish, just begging for the chance to actually cook, and landed a job at the busy *tapas* bar Bocaíto. He spotted the old television in the corner.

—Hey! We gotta see the men's 400. We won two golds today, already.

It was the summer the Games were held in Los Angeles and the American crowds were displaying patriotism bordering on dementia. Four years earlier, the U.S. had pulled out of the Moscow Games and now the Soviets had pulled out of L.A. Repercussions of all this silliness were evident in the person of Randy Blanchard. I could see the black and white images splashing on his eyeglasses. He said nothing and gulped some sherry. He had been on the men's swimming team training for Moscow when Carter pressured the Olympic Committee into withdrawing; all training was suspended. Two years later, when Randy tried out for Los Angeles, he ranked fiftieth and retired.

—At 24, man. Twelve years coached by Don Hollander. I still own all the indoor records at Stanford! And when it's my window, some cracker governor from Georgia gets sanctimonious and shuts it!

Randy had told me the story late one night at Bar Hispano. After hanging up his fins, his father had gotten him a job at Merrill Lynch in Hong Kong. But six months later Argentina invaded the Falklands. And Hong Kong, always twitchy and then a British colony, went into a financial tailspin.

—Who'd they think was sitting in 10 Downing? Mrs. Thatcher! With her pal Ronald Ray-Gun in the White House! Of <u>course</u> we hit back. Then Mrs. T upsets the Chinese over the '97 hand-over and Hong Kong finishes going to hell. They let 40 people go. I'm lucky I got this job, even if I'm not trading.

Randy had landed at Arthur Andersen, where he was bored, but Madrid gave solace while wound-licking. Mar was beautiful; dark and svelte, with waist-long black hair. She gave me the impression of having just dismounted a spirited horse.

—Plus, her painting is something she has to do alone, man. So I'm off the hook, like, six hours a day. Kevin, get yourself a girl with some solitary pursuit that doesn't make any noise. While she's in her room painting, I'm out here with Sport Magazine and Dire Straits on the 'phones.' And she considers that solidarity. Also, she hardly speaks English, which is handy when you're having a private conversation.

Randy and Mar spoke only in Spanish. He'd grown up in San Diego with Mexican servants and had an easy, if sloppy, way with the language. But he was wrong about Mar's English. I knew from Verónica, who worked with me at the ad agency, that they'd spent every summer of their youths in Ireland. In this, the Martínez-Aleya sisters were typical of upper-class Spanish women: they did not tell you everything about themselves. For me, it took some getting used to after American women's confessional/confrontational m. o.

I asked Randy how they'd met.

—At a party. She asked me to pose for her. And, where I come from, dem's <u>fuckin'</u> words.

In my case, after a serious relationship ended in New York, I hadn't really looked for anyone special in Spain. Instead, I'd focused on a new country and a new job, one I was determined to succeed at. I had gone out with a few women, all Spaniards, and that proved an education. After mastering the ground rules of American women, dating Spanish ones was like improvisational theater.

Ramón Cuevas arrived. He was a journalist who often came to our Saturday lunches and provided, as Cottie put it, *the dissenting view*. But Ramón was intelligent and extremely well-read. As they say in Spanish, he 'falls well on me'.

—Ah. Circuses for the Americans—he said, watching the braying crowds on television—. To go with all that <u>bread</u>.

Ramón was not unmindful of our slang.

—Well, you'll be seeing plenty of Americans if Barcelona hosts the '92 Games, Chaplain,—said Cottie.

Ramón smiled and slid a Ducados from his pack of cigarettes.

—That's a *catalán* problem.

—You don't seriously intend to light that thing in there, do you?—Boomed Randy's voice from the balcony.

Ramón calmly flicked his lighter.

—This is Mar's apartment. I am on Spanish soil.

Joel hurried back from the kitchen. The stuffed mushrooms bubbled with cloudlets of cheese and a fog of garlic.

—Here, eat. And where are we going for lunch, people?

—I'm busted after Pamplona. Let's go Chinese—said Cottie.

—On my first day off in two weeks?—Exclaimed Joel.

—The little Cuban place?—Ventured Cottie again.

Mar hung up the phone and declared:

—We are gheowing to La Tasca. Two-thirty reservation, so let's do harry.

—La Tasca?—Yelped Randy from the balcony—. That's 3,000 *pesetas* per person!

Mar glared at him.

—It's Saturday, it's already two o'clock. And it's the only place that would take fourteen.

—Four<u>teen</u>?—Asked Cottie.

—Yes, Barbara Isaacs is coming. So is that Dutch photographer with the model boyfriend. Oh, and the Axis Powers.—She looked at me.

My mood sagged. The Axis Powers were two Argentinian art directors at my ad agency named Marcelo Rauschenberg and Horacio Pignarelli. The German and Italian roots were the source of the nickname, but they were Argentinian nonetheless, and a little of that goes a long way.

—Hey, Ramón—Cottie asked, struck by something on the bookshelves at the other end of the living room—, all these books on Spanish history and the Spanish character; the authors are Hugh Thomas, Gabriel Jackson, Gerald Brenan, Ian Gibson and George Orwell. Your explanation, sir.

Ramón exhaled a cirrus of blue smoke and smiled.

—We have created a calling, *hispanista,* by lionizing foreign pundits and paying them to explain us to ourselves. Because we wouldn't take a Spaniard's word for anything. It would always be partisan or regional or simply personal. Conversely, we expel all our great men, the Picassos and the Casals, so you can discover them.

It was true. My philosophy professor at Bryn Mawr, Ferrater Mora, had been an exile.

Mar shut off the television and began closing balcony doors. Randy bounded back into the living room.

—Hey, listen! We won't go out. We'll order, like, thirty pizzas!

We stared at him.

—Yeah! See, they guarantee that if you don't get your order within an hour, it's free! And, well, Madrid is playing Barcelona today. All the delivery guys will be glued to the tube. They won't start delivering a thing 'til halftime. That means we'll get, like, a thousand bucks worth of pizza for nothing. It's ... it's like arbitrage!

Chapter Two

The threshold of summer in Madrid is the first week of June, when a bright green fuzz appears on the chestnut trees. Now we'd entered July, and those tea-like blossoms carried in the breeze, coating and softening the boulevard like a last souvenir of spring. The verdant flurries coincided with the book fair that clogged the Paseo del Prado with stalls and browsers, another sign of summer. As we passed the American Express office, Cottie observed:

—Now there's the real American embassy, if you ask me. Those folks can fix a problem.

—You're so right!—Added Randy—. If you get in trouble and you go to the actual embassy, they're so judgmental.

We paused at a bookstall. Ramón picked up an old paperback and looked at Cottie.

—Is your name a contraction of 'Cottard', by any chance?

—Yes. We were French once, I guess—Cottie said.

Then he saw the book Ramón was holding.

—And, no, it has nothing to do with that guy in *The Plague*. We don't read Camus in Newport.

We were meeting Barbara Isaacs, an American who wanted to break into fashion design, at the Espejo. It's a luminous, glass-enclosed café that reminds me of an old world's fair pavilion. As we reached the café, something typical of Madrid at the time occurred. Sade, the elegant African singer, glided past in an orange wrap. Simultaneously, the heartthrob of the Madrid cultural new wave known as *La Movida* asked Ramón for a light. Miguel Bosé, the epicene actor-singer, leaned into Ramón's lighter, thanked him, and moved on.

—See that, Kevin? This is a Madrid moment!—Urged Cottie.

—Madrid is being created this instant, the paint is going on the canvas, and we're the ones painting it!

Sade and Bosé had disappeared in the crowd.

—No, Cottie. They're the painters. We just watch.

Cottie became irritated.

—Kevin, I'm simply making a distinction between Madrid and, say, Paris. Paris is finished. I mean, it's done. Like a piece of pottery that's come out of the kiln. That's it, it will stay that way forever. Might as well put a velvet rope around it and charge admission.

—I believe they already do—I said.

Cottie shook his head impatiently.

—But Madrid is being invented right before our eyes. It's in constant flux, everything in a crucible. And we ... we're the <u>alchemists</u>!

—Cottie, we lit Miguel Bosé's cigarette.

Barbara Isaacs erupted out of the Espejo: almost five feet tall, with orange hair, a derby hat, a necktie and vest over a hoop skirt and Mary Janes. She was the newest arrival but, with the fervor of the converted, had embraced the anarchical Spanish fashion scene with *gusto*.

—Hiya. If we're going to Tasca's let's stop at Turner's so I can leave an ad on their bulletin board. I found a terrific apartment on Goya, but I need someone to share the rent.

Turner's was bookstore, message center, lonely-hearts club and more to a lot of us when we arrived. And it <u>was</u> on the way to La Tasca.

When we got to the restaurant, we trundled up the narrow stars to our table, which was already set with bottles of wine and baskets of bread every four places. I sat at one extreme and Ramón at the 'smokers end.' Randy and Mar sat together, as did our 'foodies', Joel and Barbara. Mar's sister Verónica sat next to me, so I was sure to get some agency gossip. Cottie picked up a wine bottle and started pouring. We were still drinking red, though once summer heated up I'd switch to white.

I studied the wine label.

—Ramón, Spain produces exactly the same things Italy and France do, and they were in the Common Market first. How's that going to work? I mean, selling this wine over there.

—The terms are indeed onerous. For Spain to sell its wine, its olive oil or its oranges in the EEC, it has to absorb 30 days of Belgium's weather, two French railroad strikes, and all of Italy's postmen.

Joel And Barbara ordered *tapas*: sizzling baby eels, plump *chistorra* sausage with oil blisters popping fragrantly in the dish, roast peppers stuffed with codfish mousse, tiny squid—flash-fried and crunchy—and a plate of aged, crumbly *manchego* cheese.

The rest of our table arrived. Simone Du Lac, a striking Belgian producer who freelanced for the ad agencies, made quite a silhouette wearing a white leotard and a turquoise cummerbund. She was very tanned and wore her hair combed back wet, framing her strong face. She looked like a *matador*. She was said to be a woman of some speed. And I was quite attracted to her.

Piet van Doornen and his companion, Jean-Luc Mondan, sat, but not together. Then came the Axis Powers, all blouse-y shirts, much wrist jewelry and bouncing black manes. Still to come were two Americans studying in Spain that summer. There was a flurry of kissing as waiters minueted around us.

—Hey, Cottie, when Wendy comes, don't start about religion. She's born-again—said Barbara.

—Born-again? She's 21! When did she have time to <u>lapse</u>?

Piet van Doornen sat opposite me. He was 6'2" and about 240 pounds, a skinhead with a face as pink as ham. But his eyes were light blue and gentle. In Holland he'd been a deejay, a cook and a bookie before discovering his talent for photography. He had shot some nice perfume ads for me in the Canary Islands. Jean-Luc was born in Algeria and had once been a top model in Paris. Head shots of him with flowing hair and Russian hats still circulated around the ad agencies but those were ten years old and Jean-Luc now worked mostly behind the camera as Piet's assistant, carrying gear.

—You know, Kevin. Ven vee got here, I vasn't sure der vud be vurk. But ve're booked all dis mont.

—*A la Movida*—We toasted simultaneously.

—Ant I hear Robert Friedlander iss moving to Madrid.

I didn't place the name.

—He vass ferry big in London once. Carnaby Street. All dat.

Jean-Luc glanced in our direction, his face taut and hollowed like an old greyhound's. He was cool to me, but, with the pragmatism of the French, always civil. Because I could give him work.

The *tapas* plates were cleared and we ordered. Mar and Verónica split a *zarzuela*, a shellfish stew (literally, an operetta) and Joel and Barbara chose the suckling pig. I wondered what the Isaacs and Marx families of New York, on a Saturday, would think about that. The Axis Powers quizzed the waiter about the beef and the veal and the lamb before ordering swordfish. Jean-Luc specified grilled sole, no sauce, thinking of some call-back he might have. Simone picked *fabada*, the bean and sausage stew. What eager appetites women here had, compared to the suspicious, unhappy way women in the States read menus. Cottie and Randy took the lamb chops and Ramón, the rabbit stew.

Piet looked at me.

—Vant to share a *cocido?*

Cocido is a gigantic pot of meats, sausages and game birds cooked for six hours with a whole orchard of things in a thick, powerful broth. It is consumed in three acts. First, the murky yellow broth, with some fine noodles; then, the boiled cabbage, potatoes, carrots, squash, onions and chickpeas with a side of garlic mayonnaise called aioli; lastly a platter groaning under a heap of the beef, pork, lamb, duck, blood sausage and *chorizo*, with a side of peppery red sauce.

—Sure.

At the other end, Ramón finished his encyclical on European unity.

—Do you know what Euro Heaven is? It's where the cooks are French, the lovers are Italian, the actors are English, the dancers are Spanish, the police are Dutch and the financiers are Swiss.

—And what is Euro Hell?—Asked Randy, playing straight man.

—It's where the cooks are English, the lovers are Swiss, the dancers are Dutch, the financiers are Spanish and the police are German.

Around five o'clock the last plates were cleared and the table swept of crumbs. Heavy cups and saucers were brought for the coffee and the cart of liqueurs and *eaux de vie* was rolled up to the table. An old woman climbed the stairs from the coatroom, carrying a half dozen boxes of cigars.

—I'm going to smoke a Havana—mused Cottie—. My father would kill for a Havana.

—And they say our generation won't live as well as our parents,—I noted.

I ordered an *orujo de yerbas*, an herb liqueur, green and jewel-y in its frost-encrusted glass. Piet had a brandy, Randy an *anís*, and the women all had a vanilla liqueur called 43. The Axis Powers, again, made the waiter recite his array of cordials before ordering J&B and soda.

Shortly everyone was ensconced in that dreamy laze called *la sobremesa*, when talk is the true meal and relationships are made (or discovered). I saw

Simone lean in to hear a whisper from Cottie. His arm was over the back of her chair. I stopped by Randy on my way to the men's room. I nodded in Cottie's direction and asked:

—How does that look?

—First and goal at the one—Said Randy, who liked sports metaphors.

When I came back, Simone was leaving and Cottie sat up, perplexed.

—What happened?—I whispered to Randy—. I thought it was first-and-goal at the one.

Randy looked at his *anís* and shrugged.

—Fumbled.

That night we went to the open-air cinema in the Retiro. The park was just a block from my place and I enjoyed it: running on the bosky paths at dawn, with a picnic and a book at lunch, and on summer nights when they showed old films. We saw *Day of the Jackal*, a favorite, though Edward Fox's voice was disconcertingly dubbed by the same announcer who did my agency's Vicks Nasal Spray spots. At any minute I expected the Jackal to demand instant relief.

The movie ended a little after midnight. Randy, Mar, Simone and I strolled along the wooden stalls that ring the movie grounds like booths at a street fair. We had San Miguel beer and *empanadillas*—baked pastries filled with tuna or sausage or cod.

—You're all welcome to come up to my place, but you'd have to sit on the floor,—I offered lamely.

—Kevin, where ees yawr furniture?—Asked Mar.

—Well, it left New York by ship in January for Panama—don't ask me why. Thence to Rotterdam. Last week the shipping agents signed for the container in Barcelona. It's now on the high roads of Spain.

—Then it's wineglasses as house-warming gifts—chimed Randy.

—Wineglasses? I'm worried about my cast-iron chair.

—Kevin, you must absolutely come with me to the flea market in the morning—entreated Simone.

—You can get wonderful old chairs for practically nothing. And dining tables, mirrors ... I furnished my place for 50,000 *pesetas*.

I tried to recall her attic on Barquillo street. I was tired of living in a cavernous apartment with only a bed, a reading lamp and a folding chair.

But though at first I missed all my belongings, I soon yearned only for my books and my colander from Ad Hoc Housewares. Lately, I'd almost become resigned to my loss and, like the children of dead parents, had begun to forget exactly what it was I'd had.

—Okay, Simone. I'll meet you there at nine.

We all said good-night and I walked on the promenade toward my place. Half a million cars had left the city, according to the paper, and the air was sweet, the sky was starry. Madrid was like one giant open-air planetarium. I walked home beneath the trees.

To get to the flea market from my place, I had to take Huertas, a street of sordid little bars that slopes downhill toward, quite usefully, the police station. On Sunday morning the steaming debris of the night emerges into the light to ponder, propped against a doorway or each other, whether to go to an after-hours bar, the disco on Gran Vía that opens at six A.M., or to get fortification at the hot-chocolate-and-cruller place on San Ginés. Bed is not an option.

I walked purposefully past a couple of these small groups in their all-black clothes, now somewhat dingy-fied by the night to a charcoal gray. One couple, a thin white man and a muscular mulatto boy, walked quickly toward me. The mulatto gave his friend a lubricious slap on the rear and cackled:

—*¿Oye, loca, tienes sueño?*

At the top of the street, near Plaza de Santa Ana, I saw a man cross the plaza wearing only an inner tube. And I rued going out so early. Ramón Cuevas said Sunday morning in Madrid made you think they'd evacuated a hospital.

I bought the Sunday paper at a kiosk and went into the café at the edge of the flea market. It wasn't nine yet but the gummy little bar already throbbed with life. Spanish Civil War cripples hit the slot machines, which played *Third Man Theme* when disgorging their coins. A florid hooker anointed herself with powdered sugar as she gouged a pastry. Two Gypsy pickpockets-cum-bootblacks ogled my wristwatch. The espresso machine hissed, cups and spoons were slammed onto saucers, and the place became a Turkish bath of cigarette smoke. I watched, then quickly turned away, as a waiter baptized the used cups in a murky tub and set them down before new customers. Cottie was right: Madrid was one great Petri dish.

—Hello, Kevin.

Simone looked, well, continental in black tights, a man's striped shirt tied off at the navel, hooped earrings and a helmet of streaked hair, slicked back. We kissed on both cheeks. She smelled fresh and grassy.

—Eau de Givenchy. It's my summer scent. Come, let's <u>buy</u>.

At the flea market, I browsed quarter-heartedly among the junk, letting Simone be my *marchande*.

—I don't feel right buying orphaned furniture.

—Previously-owned, darling, like a second-hand Rolls.

By noon I owned a green leather couch and two burgundy armchairs. Also, an oak dining table with eight cane chairs from Manila. There was a milk can, which I was assured would make a great umbrella stand, several horribly mottled mirrors (—You're buying the frames, Kevin, Art Nouveau) and a large Oriental rug which, when steam-cleaned, would look very nice. Spaniards disdain salesmanship and refuse to enhance the value of their wares if it means having to wipe a damp cloth over them. So I only spent 90,000 *pesetas* for my a-la-carte purchases at the different dealers. I paid a *transportista*, the one with the cleanest truck, to take it all to my building, where the *portero* and his son would take delivery. Then I thanked Simone and we exchanged kisses.

—Now, tonight, you open a bottle of Riscal, and you decorate!

Having some aquatic outlet in the summer is crucial in Madrid. Public pools open May 15, and some hotels will rent you a locker and a towel for a few dollars. A surprising number of people have weekend homes in Mallorca. But I liked the serenity of the private clubs. That day I'd been invited for lunch at the Real Madrid by Mercedes López-Branson, one of my clients. The club is anachronistic, with Franco-era flags and a staff that's all right-wing, down to the toiletries groom in the men's locker room. How odd that, with a socialist government in power, some workers were fascists.

Mercedes was on the terrace that overlooks the pool. She wore a white silk smock, black kung fu slippers, and an Hermès scarf tied as a bandanna. She looked like a pirate child queen. We exchanged kisses.

—Kevin, I'm not swimming today. You'll have to do your hangover laps alone.

She was half-Spanish, daughter of a Franco minister and Audrey Branson, the American movie star from the fifties. She was petite, almost pretty, with features—honey-colored hair and green eyes—that were American enough. But she had the olive skin of a Spaniard.

I changed into my bathing suit and slipped into the shallow end of the pool. The water was cool and thick and a breeze skimmed across the surface, making it like velvet rubbed the wrong way. Though I'd played baseball in school, it's not a sport you carry through life. You won't find seventeen other people to play with when you're 30. So I discovered swimming. I still ran sometimes in the morning, but I did so with grim resolve; to sweat. Swimming was indulgence, like a massage. The great length of the club's pool let me water-dream, swimming awhile before having to make the turns.

—25 laps—I announced, collapsing in a chair next to Mercedes—. I'll do more after lunch.

—They have *paella* today. You'd drown. Speaking of food, how was the Saturday *bouffe?*

—Fine. We missed you.

Mercedes looked beyond the pool to a patch of poplars.

—I can't summon the rah-rah for your lunches. I'm only half American.

—There were Spaniards.

—Only half that, too—she smiled.

—Skip it, let's get a table.

We sat under a generous pine, out of the sun. She was wary of the light. I suspected she didn't want to turn any darker than she naturally was. I pulled on an old Lawrenceville shirt without drying myself and sat down. I liked to let the water evaporate on my skin. A waiter brought two shimmering glasses of Tío Pepe and we clinked *salud*.

A woman in a black caftan came over.

—Hello, Mother. This is Kevin Byrne, from our ad agency.

—Hello, Kevin. Where are you from?

—New York. Greenwich Village.

—My, you certainly don't have an accent.

Mercedes sat back and looked at me.

—He's had it laundered at good schools. But when he talks about women or baseball, fuhgedabouddit.

—Well, I haven't been back ... must be twenty years. Anyway, I'm interrupting. Sweetie, Papa and I are flying to Jerez tonight for the horse show but I told Noufissa to fix something for you. *Besos*. Nice meeting you, Kevin.

Audrey Branson sailed off toward the clubhouse. She had to be sixty, but her skin, at least the skin around those enormous sunglasses, was smooth.

—My mother never goes back to the States. She says you can't age there.

After lunch we drifted off to lie in the grass under the poplars. A rumor of wind flowed through the leaves and I fell asleep.

Chapter Three

That Monday morning at work I had to deal with the usual suspects. Our Brazilian art director Nelson Moreira missed a flight to a photo shoot because he couldn't get his bow tie quite right. Conchi Saldaña from accounting had been the only person in the office over the weekend and now $6,000 was missing. Her mother said Conchi had not been home since Friday, but could we send any severance pay to <u>her</u>. The wife of our chief illustrator called me to say the man wouldn't make it in. He'd been in bed since Saturday.

—You understand, *Señor*, the Real Madrid lost.

After six months in Spain, I dealt with things matter-of-factly. It was easier than my last six months in New York, out of work. That last December in the city was torture by Christmas carol, death by window display. I'd walk the streets, nose dripping, getting sprayed with slush by the taxis, now mockingly available, and just poisoned with doubts about my future.

Then, in January, I was offered a job managing the Madrid office of an agency network which had never considered me for a job in the States. And so far, except for the occasional telex and a couple of calls from finance and legal, New York had left me alone. That year my Spanish financial director and I were projecting a slight profit in the plan we sent to corporate. But not enough to draw anybody's attention or justify the big boys flying over first class to loot the kitty. And with the bonhomie of a man who's recovered from a serious illness, I concluded that leaving New York was probably overdue.

My last year there had become dangerous. There was a volatility in the air; everyone I knew was scared of losing his job. People made crazy money but spent even more trying to soothe the fears. No one took vacations, lest they return to find themselves fired. Instead, we made febrile weekend sorties to Los Cabos or Mustique, returning haggard behind our tans and thousands poorer, hyperventilating in the cab from JFK to work.

It was a time when New York was a casino for careers; 24-year-olds ran departments at banks, people rented limousines to take them to restaurants ten blocks from their apartment. There was a giddy recklessness that had touches of Alice in Wonderland and the Paris Commune. When someone summoned you to his office, it could be to give you a $5,000 check and pop a magnum of Krug, or to have you escorted from the building by marshals. Even before losing my job I was feeling nauseous at work. I couldn't wait to get off and go to P.J.'s and have two glasses of wine in five minutes. An old girlfriend, also in advertising, told me she went home every night and watched the cartoon channel, without the sound, for an hour, before she could fathom doing anything else. She said:

—You know, they're coming out with a patch for smokers, so they can get a steady flow of nicotine throughout the day. I wish they'd invent a wine patch that I could wear to keep a constant three-glass level in my body.

My internal line rang.

—*El señor Chubb por la línea dos.*

—Hi, Cottie.

—Hey, there's a huge anti-NATO demonstration today at noon, down Castellana and ending up at Alcalá. They'll march right past the embassy. I think we should go take the pulse of this thing.

—Okay, I'll meet you at Bar Independencia.

I hung up and looked out at the street below. I was too new to have a feel for the anti-NATO thing. People had been marching since the weather warmed up. But I didn't know how much fervor there was out there. My secretary came in.

—May I leave early, *Señor?* I must join the march.

By the time I left the office, it was deserted. I took a cab to the state clinic on Velázquez to pick up the result of the medical exam I needed for my work permit. Spain had problems years before with Moroccan olive pickers who'd brought in TB, so now all foreign workers had to get a checkup. I'd gone to the clinic the week before, fasting and prepared to spend the day. When I got there I interrupted a card game among nurses and orderlies. One of them led me into a room with a Goldbergesque contraption and had me strip from the waist up.

—Put your chest against the steel plaque, breathe deeply and hold it.—A shrill buzzer rent the air.

—Dress and return Monday before noon.

At the clinic there was a sealed envelope with my name at the reception desk. I took a cab and headed for Alcalá to meet Cottie. In the back seat I opened the envelope. It contained a booklet, like a passport. I riffled through the pages, filled in by hand in a flowing script. The last page bore several stamps and two indecipherable signatures, along with the notary seals that alone make anything in Spain a reality. Above the signatures was this statement:

"Having examined the American Mr. Kevin Byrne, we hereby declare that he suffers no illness, physical or mental."

Well, we certainly didn't have machines like that back in the States.

The most emblematic landmark in Madrid is Plaza de la Independencia. But nobody calls it that. It's La Puerta de Alcalá, a stately multi-arched gateway in a landscaped roundabout. It is the Arch of Triumph of Spain. And cars come from all directions to circle it in what seems a choreographed tribute.

There's an outdoor café and an international newsstand facing it. I found Sunday's *New York Times*, which arrived Monday morning on the overnight flight. It was about $24. I looked at the cover story in the Sunday magazine. It was the second of a three-part article on India. I bought a *Vanity Fair*.

—Kevin! Over here!

Barbara Isaacs had staked a table on the sidewalk edge of the café; front row seats for the march.

—Barbara, mass demonstrations in Europe are not like *Les Misérables*. The mob doesn't suddenly break into song—I said.

—Mob, shmob. There. Now it's clean.

She finished cleaning the table with a Handi-Wipe and I wondered where in Spain she'd found one.

Cottie jaunted up to us.

—Good work, Barbara. Now if you could just precede me into the men's room with your cleaning kit.

—Pleez. I can't imagine the schmutz in the men's rooms here.

—Think of *Mothra Meets Mucus.*

Advance groups of marchers began arriving at the plaza walking quickly, with placards and banners. One of these had just a 'v' and 'o' on either side of the NATO logo, which in Spanish is reversed. So it read: V OTAN O, *'vote no'*. Buses from the provinces clogged Serrano street, and the police were cordoning off the area for them. In minutes, the plaza was thronged, the café was full, and the balconies above us were like theater boxes full of people. Or, as Cottie put it, six-packs with nine bottles, And there were thousands more to come, still marching, heading our way down Castellana.

But there was nothing of the brooding, combustible mood I'd felt at demonstrations back in the States. If anything, there was an effervescence in the air, as when people converge on a stadium. We ordered a bottle of sherry, almonds and a menu just as Ramón Cuevas arrived.

—Ramón, wrong pew. Aren't you in the ranks of the rabid?—Asked Cottie.

Ramón sat down and brandished his copy of *El País*, the socialist daily.

—This is my letter of transit. So I show solidarity without having to march. I detest exercise.

—Jeez, the men here are so un-muscular. They're like bialys,—observed Barbara.

It was true. Spanish men were indolent and had pale, undefined bodies under those amorphous baggy sweaters. Even in July, I hadn't seen one pair of exposed forearms.

A loud bang broke the air and hurried down Serrano toward us. Everyone looked uptown, to the embassy. After a few seconds, when we saw no smoke and heard no sirens, people went back to being in the demonstration or watching it. Our drinks came. Now the plaza really was jammed. A makeshift platform had been erected on the roundabout.

But those milling on it had only one loudspeaker, which they passed around awkwardly, trying their hand at urgent, spontaneous calls to action. The sound did not carry and they shortly climbed down. Around two-thirty, the demonstration came undone, placards went facedown over trash cans, banners were furled and shoved into cars and buses, and in the clusters of people around us, discussions were largely about where to eat. I was to see many demonstrations in Madrid and throughout Spain, for many different causes. And none would ever be equal to the dispersive powers of lunch.

We ordered *tapas* and spent time enjoying the view, until the barricades were removed and traffic flowed once more around the Gate of Alcalá. Around five o'clock, I said goodbye and started walking home. When I got there, I found a note from my housekeeper:

—*Señor*, a man called. Your furniture is here.

Simone ordained that Saturday's lunch be at my place. My furniture had just arrived and I had the largest apartment. That morning I watched small, dour Manola command the blue-bristled men in elephant-minder overalls as they brought in the crates I hadn't seen in six months. Opening them would be a mix of Christmas and *Truth or Consequences*. Simone had come to help and, as the last crate was brought in, told me I shouldn't deal with the what-goes-where and sent me out for flowers and food.

I was glad to miss the unveiling of my cargo. Simone would know intuitively where to put things. I strolled up Serrano to Castañer and saw the flowers just in from Amsterdam. I ordered a dozen stargazers for the living room, a dozen yellow tulips for the dining room, and some tuberoses for my bedroom. The florist said he'd throw in some new eucalyptus and I went off to the market.

As usual, I had no menu in mind. But when I saw the sea urchins and their gleaming roe, I wanted to do a seafood soup as a first course. I bought two bags of mussels, three spiny lobsters, a kilo of prawns, fresh cod, rockfish, scallops and crab. Then I found a butcher who de-boned two legs of lamb, which I would roast and serve with a potato gratin and a salad. Since it was a sort of housewarming, I ordered a case of Spanish champagne to be sent home, where I hoped my wineglasses were being, at that moment, successfully unwrapped.

When I eventually got there, the kitchen was strewn with cardboard, newspaper, and Styrofoam pellets. Manola's face was salted with dust and her hair had wood shavings for ringlets; she looked oddly like Harpo. The doorman and his wife had been added to the team and I began to calculate tips for all. Simone was in a corner, holding a Baccarat flute brimming with champagne.

—Kevin, this is arduous. And people will be here in two hours. They just brought up the flowers, so I'll get started with those. Why don't you get busy with the cooking?

A few moments later, a Brazilian *samba* (music I did not own) flowed through the place from the stereo. Simone had somehow managed to wire my set to the European system. I went to work happily, rediscovering my Sabatier knives, my stockpots, and my beloved colander.

—You know, these plates are beautiful—Barbara was saying four hours later—. They're the ones they have a Le Moulin; it's a three-star.

—And at El Amparo, right here in Madrid—added Simone.

—And where do you get your lettuce?—Asked Joel.

—Ayala's.

—That man—said Joel, looking heavenward—, is the Cartier of produce.

Manola had postponed her noon exit to stay and help. Now she was serving champagne, tentatively, around the table where twelve of us had somehow managed to find a place. My wine glasses had all made the trip safely, though tougher pieces had succumbed. Simone put on Linda Ronstadt just as Joel clinked a wine bottle with his spoon. He stood for the *pronunciamiento*.

—First of all, the seafood soup was a triumph, using urchin roe as a thickener. Sure beats cornstarch, darling. Now, the lamb ... I dunno about lamb in the summer.

Some groaned at the table and Joel put his palms up.

—Still, still; juicy, lustrous. And the gratin! Was that Julia's?

We lingered until we simply had to get up. I opened the balconies, one for Randy and Mar, and one for the smokers. Ramón was eyeing stacks of books on the floor, which I would be putting on the shelves for the next few days. Some were textbooks from prep school I'd forgotten about. Half of them, like some of my clothes and a few of the kitchen utensils, I could have sworn were somebody else's.

Barbara Isaacs was photographing Simone's floral arrangements.

—These would make fabulous silkscreens on sundresses!

Mar came in from the balcony.

—Kevin, we have to decide about Mallorca. We can't wait 'til Awe-goost; everyone in Spain is going because the royal family's there and they've invited Princess Diana.

—How much is it?—Asked Cottie.

—67,000 *pesetas* per person, two to a room for five days. Cottie, that's cheap.

While Cottie thought about it, Barbara and Joel agreed to share a room. Simone begged off—she had to go to Belgium. Ramón explained he was anti-monarchy and 'anti-sand'. So I offered to share with Cottie.

—I'd take Kevin up on it, Cottie. I don't think you can find a friend in two weeks—said Randy.

—How long is the flight from Madrid?—Asked Barbara.

—Fifty-five minutes—said Mar.

Barbara pawed the air.

—Aw, like the Boston-New York shuttle.

I suddenly remembered something. Linda Ronstadt's *Cry Like a Rainstorm* wailed from the living room and I sang along as I went down the hall for my date book.

—Guys, I'll have to meet you there. I have to see a client in Jerez and then go to London. I'll fly to Mallorca from there.

Simone was on the balcony having one her rare cigarettes.

—So, you're going to London?—She said, smiling.

No one else knew about London and about Alice.

Chapter Four

You knew it was August. The green blooms on the trees had long since ripened into chestnuts and the leaves drooped, curling at the edges with heat rust. A hot current blew into the night and the few people left in the city stayed indoors. Madrid then was delightful; you could get a parking space, a table at a restaurant, and theater tickets. I enjoyed it briefly. I had to fly to Jerez.

Andalucía in summer is like an Arab state. Merchants drop large dusty canopies over their shops. Dates hang listless from their palms. Stray dogs skip along deserted streets. But my sherry client had granted me an audience before closing the distillery for three weeks.

Don José Sánchez Cubero was the seventh-generation owner of the largest sherry producer in the world. He saw me at the bodegas in the port of Santa María where thousands of his casks awaited the ships that would take them, mostly to England. It was a hot day but in the *cortijo* of the main building it was cool and quiet. Don José sat at a table with a mosaic top. He wore a white shirt, loose khaki pants and espadrilles. His face was gnarled like an olive tree.

Two white-gloved waiters came into the courtyard. One poured him a cold glass of sherry. The other served filmy slices of cured ham, lustrous and mahogany-hued, and the unique striped prawns of Sanlúcar. Don José began to peel one and waved it at me. I launched my pitch.

—There are seven wine-producing countries in the Common Market. But only Spain makes authentic sherry. If we marketed it throughout the continent, we would be unopposed.

For five minutes Don José allowed me to preach and propose while he shelled his shrimp and popped olives like peanuts. New glasses of fresh cold sherry appeared just as he drained the one in his hand. But his hooded old eyes never left my face. I came to a halt just as he gulped down another sherry and wiped his hands on his pants, ignoring the silver finger bowl held out to him. Then, almost drowsily, he began his reply to me, ruminating on something I was sure he had already concluded, perhaps many years before.

—Now, you want me to market my sherry abroad. That means increasing production for the new demand, planting new vines or buying someone's vineyard; and then more machinery, and hiring more people. And that means going to the banks for financing and to the unions to negotiate the personnel issues. Then I must visit these countries to find partners, distributors, and local lawyers to protect my copyright ...

He took a proffered cigarette from the tray and it was lit for him.

—... Print labels in many languages. And, of course, invest in advertising to educate the Germans and the Dutch and the rest. But, let me ask you something. If I do all that your propose ...

He paused to sip from a new glass of sherry. A white thoroughbred came into the courtyard. Two Moorish grooms helped Don José's new 30-year-old bride dismount. Swallows trilled in the sun and the fountain murmured happily.

—... Are you telling me that I will live any better?

From Jerez to London the flights are full in first class with Spanish gentry going to England to hunt. Coach is empty, except for a few sunburned Brits returning to the industrial north after their week in the sun.

I went straight to Blakes Hotel, in a mews-y street of South Kensington, and up to my usual room, #208. The concierge sent up some cassettes he thought I might like during my visit: Memphis Slim, the Julie London tape with *Cry Me a River* and *The Nearness of You*, and a new group called Communards. I slipped Julie into the machine, and looked over the telexes and phone messages they gave me at the desk. I went into the pantry and got a split of champagne. I took it back to the sofa, sat down, swigged straight from the bottle, and dialed Alice. She answered on the second ring.

—Hello Alice, I'm in London.

—So am I.

—Alice, I only meant ... that I'm here. If you want to have dinner.

—Are you staying at Blakes? Of course you are. Because it's three blocks from my house.

—No. I stay here because it's nice and the company allows it.

—Well ... I can have dinner, but not late.

—Alice, I live in Spain, but I don't have to have dinner at midnight. How about Tante Claire?

—We'll never get a table. Blakes is good, and you're a guest, so they have to seat you. I'll be there in thirty ... in an hour.

As it happened, the hotel restaurant was excellent: few tables in a cool art deco setting, wonderful eclectic food and clientele. It's the only place you'd find both David Frost and David Bowie.

As I showered I thought about the winding ways that had brought Alice Kariatydis and me to Europe. She was the only woman I'd ever lived with; in a duplex on 20th Street while we both worked at the same ad agency. She was intelligent, funny, a sensual woman with salt-and-pepper hair and lots of Navajo jewelry. She was ten years older than I. And she was my boss. Well, had been. It began one day at the bank on the ground floor of our agency in New York, when I made a flip, puerile comment.

—Hey, boss, still married? Don't worry, these things take time.

Three weeks later, the receptionist told me Alice's husband had left her. I felt like a hit-and-run driver. She stayed home for about a week, while a messenger took her work. One Friday, I bought Jarlsberg, *paté*, and a loaf of pumpernickel and bribed the messenger to take it uptown. Just as I was leaving, my phone rang.

—Thanks for the supplies. But I'm not an invalid, you know.

—Still. It's from Balducci's. You don't have that uptown.

—What do you call Zabar's, chopped liver?

—Well, yes. Anyway, if you need anything ...

—I'm out of wine, actually. And the store just closed.

I winced. Friday at rush hour, I'd have to go up forty blocks, and then cross the entire West Side to Riverside Drive.

—Stay right there.

When she opened the door I saw a foyer with blown-up photos of Masai mounted on the wall. Kim Carnes cried out from within. The red sunset on the river was in my eyes, making her a silhouette.

—Well, these new delivery boys <u>are</u> cute. Speak English?

She went off with the bottles of Riserva Ducale. It was a huge apartment, pre-war, and the living room was separated from the dining room by two doors made from stained glass windows. The sofa was a long black velvet and teak piece from the thirties. The tall windows faced the Hudson and we were on the fifteenth floor, so the barges glided by silently on the copper water.

We talked for two hours. Or I talked, mostly. About work, of course, and about travel—the lot she'd done and the little I had. About New York, where we'd both been born, and about Seven Sisters schools, where we'd both gone. I told her I was sorry about her marriage. And I think I said I admired her, and how I liked working for her. Maybe I was just a 26-year-old with a belated crush on a teacher. But in New York City, in 1981, you didn't bring an apple. So we drank the wine and I sat there talking, trying to charm this wise woman with the big Greek eyes and the ivory necklace and the swinging breasts and the Vassar brains. I had been talking for a while when she took the glass from my hand, put it on the table, and said:

—I have a headache from not kissing you.

The sunset burned into the bedroom, staining the peach walls crimson and making everything give up its scent. The paint on the windowsill, the book by the bed, a wilting iris. I could smell them all. And her: warm, cinnamon-colored smells. Leather on her neck, autumn leaves under her arms. Her breasts hung above me and her nipples tasted of cocoa. Her face was lost in a jungle of curls and I pulled her to me, licking the oily cedar of her forehead while my hands pressed her harder to me, and me into her. Then we were tasting each other and it was like undertow—the flavor, and not knowing if the seabed was above or below. And I went further along with my tongue along her ripeness all the way back to where it's like old roses.

Blakes' dining room was full, so I got a table in the Oriental reading room, just off the bar. Alice was exactly ten minutes late, to show she owed me no consideration. She came down the stairs from the lobby in a flowing linen dress and wearing much Mediterranean jewelry. Her hair was less black but her skin was alive and her eyes were big and liquid as black olives. I hadn't seen her in a year.

We kissed on both cheeks. She looked me over before sitting down.

—Hmm. Earth tones. Spain do that to you?—Alice was very aware of dress.

—My maid did it to me. It's what she packed.

She ordered a kir, and I a martini. I could see Peter Ustinov at the bar.

—So ...—I began.

—Work's fine, health's fine, London's fine. Next.

I shook my head in what I hoped was a good-natured way.—Alice, my questions are not perfunctory.

—Okay. I'm worried about my job. I'm seeing a married man, and I might be pregnant, damn it.—She took a long sip of my martini—. How's Spain?

—Getting good. Summer's nice.

—Taking any hols?—Her anglicisms weren't an affectation. She really was saying things like 'shedule' naturally now.

—I'm flying to Mallorca tomorrow.

—Only civil servants go there, Kevin. Wool socks and sandals on the beach. Pipe smokers looking for a pub with the Arsenal-United game. We went to Santorini. What's happened?

—Well, Alice, that trip was heavily subsidized by my boss at the time.

We ate silently to knives and forks skating over Wedgwood. Finally, she sat back in her chair and put her napkin down.

—You're 29, aren't you?—She flung at me, accusingly—. I just turned 40!

I was about to congratulate her, but reconsidered.

—You could have come here to live with me.

—You had the job in London, Alice. I didn't.

—And you preferred to be out of work in New York to letting me support you here.

—Actually, yes.

She took a quick sip of Chablis, swept her shawl back over one shoulder and stood.

—You ... can stand this. The dinners, the small talk. And I can't.—She left.

Upstairs, Communards' *Don't Leave Me This Way* galloped through the suite. I opened a small bottle of calvados. The phone rang.

—Will you come over, Kevin? Will you, please?

Chapter Five

From the air, Mallorca's cathedral looks computer-generated, an improbable Gothic juggernaut for a rustic island. It overlooks the capital, Palma, a raffish port city with more sidewalk menu boards in German and English than in Spanish, and where wandering Levantines blend with topless Stockholm secretaries on the narrow streets. The harbor is also home to the U.S. Navy's Sixth Fleet, so the nightlife is predictably louche. All of this makes the cathedral even more incongruous.

But the interior of the island and the craggy coast are cleansed, and the water in the coves is gem-like. Byron and Graves made this home, and there is a spartan Greekness to it—honey-colored rocks and tufty, fragrant bushes twisted by the wind. After three days there, my Madrid persona washed off. I discovered the visceral joys of walking barefoot, wearing linen, and tasting salt on my skin. I went for long swims twice a day, and walked along the cliffs, just breathing the oxygenated air that was pumped into me up there. It was the fifteenth of August, high point of summer, and I was young and I was in Spain.

That morning we'd gone diving and Randy brought back a starfish for Barbara, who declared it the design motif of the future, or at least <u>her</u> future.

—Not just clothes—furniture, jewelry, hood ornaments for cars!

—And ratings for seaside hotels. Ours would be a two-starfish place,—said Cottie as his eyes wandered over the newspaper, not getting any traction.

—Cottie, when are you going to learn Spanish?

—I have one word for you, Counselor: *piano*. Eight years of piano. Said it would open up worlds for me. I figure I missed about 2,000 games of tennis. So don't tell me about Spanish. Here. Just translate the headlines.

The lead story was about the royal family and fears of an attempt on the king's life, following the arrest of Basque terrorists.

—What do these terrorists want, anyway?—Asked Barbara.

—To terrorize—said Mar, flatly.

We had a lunch at Rocamar, a place at the marina.

—You know, Joel, I can't have the lobster today. I woke up with a vita-min deficiency—said Randy, eyeing the menu.

—Which vitamin?—Asked Joel.

—Vitamin 'M', replied Randy, rubbing thumb and forefinger together.

—So have the grilled sardines. Just 500 *pesetas*. And get the fried pota-toes, they're big as two-by-fours.

Just then, a striking blond man approached the table. He was so tanned and his eyes were so light, he looked almost like a photographic negative.

—Kevin? Jeff Rakes. I was the boyfriend in your coffee commercial.

—Sure. The spot turned out well. Join us for lunch?

—There's a chair here,—said Barbara, smiling up at him.

After lunch, Jeff went over to the marina to see about renting a boat.

—Jeez, what a hunk. Where do you think men like that hang out?

—At their Spanish girlfriends' apartments—offered Cottie.

—Gimme a break. I don't get that Spanish women are different. Noth-ing personal, Mar.

—Well, they are—said Randy—. If an American girl had been trying to find me all day with no luck, she'd say:

—Where the hell have you been?

—A Spanish girl would offer me a drink and say:

—Tell me about your day.

Jeff came back.

—I've got that sailboat. It'll hold two more people.

Cottie and I joined him in the skiff. It was a hot day, but the whitecaps sprayed us with cool brine. We headed for the northern part of the island, making good time along the coast.

—An awesome sight is the cliff at Cabo Formentor. It comes right out of the sea. Great swimming there.

Jeff knew the island.

—Isn't the water a little rough?—I asked.

—There's some chop at the base. But we'll go out, half a mile.

As we neared the cape, strong currents took us and I wondered about taking that swim.

Then we were in sight of it, a majestic rock going up in the air; a primordial thing.

—What did I tell you?

We lowered the anchor about a thousand yards from the cliff. The water was inky blue with some pockets of green, like mint jelly. I heard a splash behind me. I looked over the bow and saw jade-green bubbles coming up.

Jeff broke the surface and tilted his delighted face back.

—It's fabulous! You go through a warm zone and then a patch that's ice-cold. Come on in!

A few minutes later, we were all whooping happily in the water. It felt thick and cold and I had to keep moving just to stay in place. The cliff was in shadow and forbidding. I could hear the waves crash at the base, sending rivers of foam a hundred feet up the rock.

That night we all went to Kul, the disco du jour. It was in the heart of town and all the city's constituencies flowed to it. At the entrance were a bouncer stuffed into a tuxedo, two Civil Guards with machine guns, and a pair of black American MP's. The building breathed with the seismic beat of the music inside. We went up the to the second-floor bar for drinks. Downstairs, *One Night in Bangkok* thumped away.

—I love this song—cooed Joel, and he led Barbara away.

We ordered vodka *limón* all around. I looked at myself in the mirror behind the bar. My sun-beaten face looked back, red and revitalized. Suddenly I smelled a green vitamin in the air, new and citric. It was Jeff. He wore a white linen jacket over a black tee shirt. He was still shower-wet and his face just gleamed. I bought him a drink and asked if he had jobs coming up.

—I have a ten-day shoot—all fashion stuff—in Barcelona. The pay's not great, but I get to keep some clothes—he said.

—Well, you've got the right look.

He sipped his drink.

—In Spain I do. It's not very unique back in California. But advertisers here want beach boys. Same thing in Japan, I worked there for six months. That's how I paid for my apartment here.

Barbara and Joel came back.

—I met the strangest woman. She gave me her card. She's a real-state agent here. But she's English.

—That must be Astrid Hippisley-Coxe—Jeff said—. She's famous. Hangs out looking for tourists. She talks them into looking at apartments and bungalows. People go to indulge a fantasy.

—Does she sell many apartments?

Jeff laughed.

—Sold me mine.

Downstairs, *Caribbean Queen* began its silly tale.

—Excuse us—said Randy, as he was led away by Mar.

—I'll wait for a Cole Porter number—called out Cottie as they walked off.

Jeff and I went down to the dance floor and blended into the crowd during an aerobic version of *Venus*. I danced indistinctly with a redhead, a Spanish couple, and by myself. But Jeff was petitioned by a blonde in a white tank top and mini-skirt. She was very brown, with leonine hair and long dark legs. When the Go-Go's began hurling *We Got The Beat*, I decamped for a refill. Joel was at the bar.

—Hi. Where's Barbara?

—Well, I think she and I had a dance-partner conflict.

Through a large glass dome I could see down into the dance floor and I spotted Barbara's orange curls. She was dancing with a stylish kid in Vietcong pajama bottoms.

Joel drained his vodka *limón* and put the glass down.

—Well, see you back at the hotel.—He left.

Cottie reappeared.

—Why'd Joel look so down?

I pointed out Barbara and the young dancer.

—Hmm. Do you think our Joel is *de l'autre équipe*?

Jeff appeared, flushed and beaming, and asked for two refills.

—Just came for fuel ... she's half-Arab, half-Italian, with a suite at the Meliá. She smells like Heaven. And, God, what a dancer!

He had shed his jacket and his shirt was damp. He took the drinks.

—Now, guys, I'm not deserting you. But I think this is on the menu. So if we split, remember we're still on for tomorrow, noon sharp at the marina for a reprise of Formentor!

He toasted us with the glasses and slinked off to beat of the music. Cottie and I watched as Jeff reappeared on the dance floor and handed the girl a drink.

—Think I can go down there, cut in and steal away Miss Thunder Thighs? I was on the chess team at Dartmouth. That might sway.

A few minutes later, we watched Jeff leave with the girl. We stayed until two and walked back to the hotel. The promenade was fragrant with orange blossoms and sea, a scent I'd always match with Mallorca. Back in the room, Cottie fell asleep while I read Maugham stories. Around three o'clock, there was a knock on the door. It was Barbara.

—Joel's not back yet.

—Well, this is the home of the Sixth Fleet,—said Cottie without stirring.

—You're horrible. Still, why should Joel get upset because I danced with some other guy?

—Because Joel probably wanted to dance with him, too—I said.

—Well, it's hard enough competing with other women for the guys out there. Don't tell me I have to also compete with men.

—Well, if it's any consolation, the only one whose social life improved tonight is Jeff.

—Figures. What did she look like? No, don't tell me. My room's on the tenth floor and those reefs down there would Cuisinart me.

I stayed up for another hour and finished my Maugham. I looked out the window. The sea was black and white under the moon. And I watched the foam make filigrees on the rocks below.

In the morning Cottie and I went to the marina to meet Jeff. We waited until two o'clock, when Cottie declared lunchtime.

—You know—said Cottie, wagging a French fry at me—, even if the guy won the damn lottery, he shouldn't stand up his friends and make them wait in the sun for two hours.

At four o'clock, just as I was going to take a nap at the hotel, the phone rang.

—Kevin … it's Jeff … I'm hurt.—His voice was faint and parched.

—Where are you?

—Meliá … her room. But she's gone an …—He began coughing.

—Jeff, listen to me: Where's your wallet? Look for your keys.

—No clothes ... I'm here on the floor ... just a big towel wrapped around me, tight ... and ... oh my God ... oh my God ... I'm leaking blood!

—Jeff! What's the room number?!

—I don't know ... I ... I think I'm going to faint.

—Jeff!!! Look on the phone dial! What's the number???

—204 ...

The line went dead.

I called the Meliá and had to tell the clerk twice before he sensed this was no tourist's prank. Then I bolted out the door, down the stairs, through the lobby, and jumped into the front seat of the first cab.

The Meliá was ten minutes away and the ambulance was already there. I got off the elevator on the second floor and was stopped by a cop. The hallway was full of people and a few bystanders in bathing suits. I explained who I was and made my way into the room.

Jeff was lying on a gurney, unconscious. He was white. On the floor I saw the hotel towel, soaked black with blood. Jeff's midriff was heavily bandaged and a medic was rigging an i-v drip over him.

He shook his head.

—Third time this season. Same gang, I bet. From the Middle East. That's where the money is. But your friend's lucky. They only took one kidney.

On the plane back to Madrid, no one said much. We were all sunburned but looked more contused than tanned. My shirt already seemed loud and there was sand in my shoe. I looked out the window as the island left us. It was just a big rock in a gray and snarly sea.

When we landed in Madrid that evening, Simone was at the airport, unexpectedly.

—Kevin, your housekeeper called me. Someone broke into your flat.

My front door had been hacked off its hinges and the frame had separated from the wall. It must have been a noisy affair. Then again, all the tenants were out of town and my *portero* lived in the basement and didn't hear all that well. My maid had been so shaken up when she came to water the plants that she hadn't even entered the place. Simone and I went in quietly. The living room and dining room had not been touched, nor had my study. We went down the hall and I noticed the pictures on the wall were askew.

—Looking for a wall safe—whispered Simone.

It was in my bedroom that I confronted the break-in. The bed had been stripped and the mattress sliced lengthwise. So had the pillows, and the room was like a bombed chicken coop. The dressing mirror was broken in three pieces and looked vaguely like a Magritte. All the drawers in my dresser had been spilled on the floor. And in my closet, the suit bags had been slashed.

—Can you tell what's missing, Kevin?

—Well, my spare watch. It was a Santos, but an old one. And I think ... yeah, I can't find the cufflinks Alice gave me.

—Oh, no ... the gold ones with the yin-yang dolphins?

—Yep.

—Look, Kevin: you can't stay here. I don't mean just tonight. Your place has been violated. Let the *portero* and your housekeeper worry about it. Who knows when they'll get a new door? Come, take the clothes you need and we'll go to my place. And bring your suitcase from Mallorca, we'll wash it all.

15 Barquillo Street is unique: in the heart of old Madrid, a red-brick tower like an American college dorm. It's familiar to young arrivals: small kitchens and clean baths, living rooms like squash courts. It was everyone's first home in Madrid, a holding pen until you decided whether you stayed.

Simone had one of the attics; a cozy one-bedroom with a living/dining room under a sloping skylight. It was neat and tasteful, with a couple of fine pieces—a Gobelin on the floor and some *cloisonné* on the mantle—that did not come from any flea market. Then I recalled her father was somebody in Brussels.

She took my suitcase from Mallorca and opened it next to the washing machine. As the island-wear piled up, tired and damp, I was reminded of how streamers and hats look the morning after a party. She slapped a lever on the machine.

—There. Now let's get some dinner.

It was almost ten. I stood there. Then she came close. She took my face in her hands.

—Come on, Kevin—she kissed my mouth—. You're home.

We went to the Peruvian place. I guess we didn't feel like running into anybody. And we ordered *pisco* sours.

I told her about Jeff, of course. And Joel's night of pout.

—Well, darling, he's gay as a beach ball. They get that way.

We ordered two more rounds of *pisco* sours, tart and frothy, before looking at the menu.

—So, how was Belgium?

Simone looked down at her drink.

—Messy. I ran into my husband.

She'd never told me she was married. She smiled.

—It's nothing. André was rich and I was eighteen. He was my father's business partner. Still is, actually. Anyway, I'm so glad to be back in Madrid. Summer never really got to Belgium this year. It was kind of drippy and <u>so</u> much time indoors. I envy your tan. *Bien bronzé*. And your hair's lighter.

—It'll soon be white if I have any more scares.

She laughed.

—Oh, Kevin, come on. That's life; more than that—that is <u>living</u>! That is why we're in Spain. Do you want to go back to America? Do I want to live in Belgium? Is your country good because it has Medicare? Or is mine, because people respect stop signs?

She drained her glass and leaned across the table, inches from my face.

—Look, Kevin, Spain isn't very sane and it isn't very safe, but this is the ride I want a ticket to. I want a country that shouts, not one that sleeps. A country that rages, that … <u>spills</u> things! Kevin, we get <u>one</u> canvas in life. We can't ponder the blank space too long before we start painting. I want <u>Spain</u> to paint me now, while I'm young. I want the finished portrait of Simone Du Lac to show it. When I'm old I want people to say—what a 'lovely life'; and part of what they will love will be the years that Spain painted on me. What do you want on your canvas: The Reagan years?

Sobering thought.

—Kevin, none of us paints the canvas alone.—She reached for my hands—. Sometimes you have to trust someone with the brush.

Back at her place, we were kissing on the floor. We were gasping but our mouths stayed pressed and I held her tighter as we rolled off the carpet and into a Chinese screen. Her hand hooked the top of my shirt and pulled down hard. Buttons sprinkled on the floor. I pulled at her snug leotard and she helped me slide it down. She eased out of it and lay flat, looking up at me, hard of breath. An upturned lamp was making sudden shapes on the wall and I got on my knees to undo my belt and she let her naked legs go out to either side of me. Then she started caressing herself, around her nipples and in her mound and I wanted her urgently. I slipped off my pants and she reached for me, took me hard and pulled me into her. She let out a gasp and I drove in further.

—*Vite, au fond*—she moaned.

Chapter Six

By September everyone in the city was back at work. Projects came to us in a full-court press and I began a frenzied round of trips and meetings and new-business presentations, so I hadn't seen much of anybody for a while.

One Saturday I hosted the lunch at my place. It was getting cool and I wanted comfort food. I decided to make *moussaka*. Maybe I was thinking of Alice. I'd gotten a letter that morning but hadn't opened it.

Two new people came. Cottie brought a girl from the embassy's commercial section and Piet called to say he'd be coming with Robert Friedlander, the English photographer.

I followed the familiar steps of the sublime Elizabeth David recipe and made it oven-ready. Then I slathered the *baguettes* of garlic bread and put them aside. Manola was making a copious Greek salad. I was cheating on dessert, ordering *baklava* by phone from a Lebanese baker. The night before, I made stuffed vine leaves and *taramasalata*. I'd also found six bottles of retsina, the varnish-y wine that needs to be the temperature of Freon before you can get it down. But we could ignore it and drink Riscal.

There were ten for lunch and I was glad to see Joel and Barbara, gossipy and close. Randy came, but Mar was off preparing her first gallery show. Cottie brought his guest, Simone came alone, as did Ramón. Piet arrived last, with Robert Friedlander.

Simone helped me in the kitchen, making drinks and garnishing the appetizers. She saw the letter from London.

—Afraid to open it?

I'll open it at work on Monday, when I'm busy.

Simone came over and ran a finger down my forearm.

—Kevin, maybe that's a road you haven't reached the end of.

—I think it would be more of a detour now.

She smiled.

—You're too young to be discarding. And I hope you wouldn't do it for my sake.

We had not made love again since the night at her place. We were physically at ease with each other, even affectionate, but sex seemed somehow remote.

In the living room Randy was puzzling over something the girl from the embassy said.

—Now let me get this. You work in the commercial section; promoting U.S. goods and companies in Spain.

Cottie and I looked at each other. When Randy was 'cross-examining', he was fierce, 6'4", and a very wide wing span beating in the young woman's face. Her name was Nancy Kroll and she was different from the usual *debs-and-daughters-of* at the embassy; girls who'd majored in Aspic and Molds at places like Sophie Newcombe.

She looked earnest, in her pleated skirt and turtleneck. She was a <u>believer</u>.

—That's right. I go around Spain, spreading the good word.

Randy made a full turn in the room, thumbs positioned behind invisible suspenders.

—Now, then, tell us what, from our infinite American bounty, do you promote? Cars? Computers? Boeing airplanes, Kellogg's Corn Flakes? Maybe the Slinky Toy or the Pet Rock?

If Mar had been there, this would not be happening, because Randy wouldn't be on his fourth sherry.

—Well, my assignment is to promote California olives.

I shut my eyes. Simone barely suppressed a laugh.

Randy's eyes widened.

—So you're pushing an expensive commodity on the world's number-one, primo-quality, thousand-specie, cheap-as-dirt purveyor of said commodity? Confess, Nancy Kroll, you are in the CIA.

Lunch was pleasant. I sat next to Robert Friedlander, a tall snowy man with a medieval haircut and a goatee. He spoke in a soft Oxbridge accent.

—I've found a studio. Reminds me of my first in Soho, oddly enough.

—Do you plan to do commercial work?

He threw his head back and laughed like a Saxon earl.

—I will be ecstatic to do commercial work. In fact, I am now, shamelessly calling on <u>you</u> for work.

—I'd love to see your book. Anything I'd know?

He took a sip of Riscal, stroked his goatee and peered over my shoulder into the living room.

—Given your age and nationality, and the fact you still have long-playing records on your shelves, I would guess I shot the record covers on two of those albums.

I stared at him, then at Piet, who'd been watching this exchange with amusement. Friedlander raised his long body from the table and went over to the record cabinet, humming something. He was wearing a dark green leather jacket with a pointed-collar shirt. He looked like an older Robin Hood. He came back to the table.

—Actually, you own three of my album covers.—He placed them before me.

I didn't check the photo credits. No one would falsely claim them, when you're talking about the most famous band in history.

—I was friends with them. And it was all a long, long time ago.

I suppose that's how we ended up listening to the records and singing along with them. It was eight o'clock when I noticed the carpet in the living room was strewn with old LP's. We could have been in our parents' basements, back in the States, many years before, sitting around innocently still, and safe.

The light outside was starting to go and I got up to close the balconies.

—Why don't we stretch our legs … before it gets dark?

—Yeah—Barbara spoke up—. I want to get one more *horchata*, the last one of the summer.

She meant the fresh seasonal drink that's like almond milk. We walked out of my building into a blue-and-magenta evening. A sudden gust blew through the trees. Chestnuts cascaded onto the sidewalk, ricocheting like gunshots and staining the street. It suddenly felt cold.

—Guys, I'll catch up with you.

I went back upstairs, through the kitchen to the storage room and found the New York box that was still uncrated. I needed a sweater.

AUTUMN
(Two years later)

Chapter Seven

The park in autumn was a bit sad, but in a pretty kind of way. The paths were carpeted with leaves no one would sweep, birds huddled on mossy statues, and the rowboats were all moored because kids were back at school. But the air was wet and bracing and you could hear the fountains murmur just for you.

I took my dogs there on their first birthday. I never thought I'd get a dog in Spain, let alone two, but it was a way of deciding what I was going to do; as Simone would say, a way of painting my canvas. Besides, my labs were special.

—Very rare—said the Irish breeder—. Their mum was a chocolate lab, don't you know, so they've got chocolate eyes and muzzle, but yellow coats.

The day was blustery and big pieces of sky shifted like stage flats. I unleashed the dogs and they took off like cheetahs. A hundred yards off people talked while their dogs romped and circled and jumped. Mine pulled up short and, with tails wagging furiously, looked for a way into the scene.

Then they plunged into the roiling choreography while the humans remained aloof, except for a stroke or an ear-rub, dispensed to any dog demanding it, regardless of whose it was.

I caught up with the group. My dogs ran over to claim me and to show they'd made the site secure.

—They're beautiful—said an older woman in riding clothes—. Are you going to show them?

—Some manners, maybe.

—What are their names?

—Pan and Vino.

At home there was a letter from Simone. She liked the picture of the dogs and said she was close to getting a job with a TV station. But New York was very competitive.

—You were right about things. Everything, actually. But tell Joel there's not one *tapas* bar in all Manhattan. Stay well and know this is your home. Please visit.

Simone had been in Madrid four years, so she'd *graduated*. And New York was a place she'd always wanted to *do*. She had just turned 25.

Mercedes López-Branson called to invite me to the club. It was the last day the pool would be open and we'd have it to ourselves. In the back of a cab I read the *Tribune* and realized the World Series started in a week, but there was nowhere in Spain to watch. It was the third year in a row I'd miss it.

I did five laps in the chilly water, but the sun was a pale yolk and warmed no more, so I got out and wrapped myself in a towel. The poplar leaves had turned a silvery gray and fluttered like Mylar.

At table I poured two glasses of Siglo red and we toasted. Mercedes was no longer my client. Her company had merged and now used another agency, but we kept in touch. I talked about work and trips I'd made. Suddenly, she asked:

—Kevin, why have you never asked me out? I mean, we no longer have a professional ... conflict or anything.

—Um ... it never ... I just haven't gotten around to it, I guess.—She came closer.

—It's okay ... really ... it's just that Spanish men find me too independent or something. And Americans think I've gone native. I thought maybe you ... look, my mother's being honored at a film festival in San Sebastián on Sunday. Wanna go?

San Sebastián is the most genteel city in Spain.

—I'd love to.

Then I remembered I had to be in Paris Monday morning.

—So, we'll drive to Paris from San Sebastián after the ceremony Sunday night.

—Mercedes, my meeting's at eight in the morning.

She smiled and shrugged.

—Some other time.

Sunday night at Le Bristol in Paris I dined alone and went upstairs at eleven. I watched the news, left a wake-up call and fell asleep. The phone woke me at three A.M. It was the concierge.

—*Monsieur* ...—the voice was calm and sure—a young woman, *Mademoiselle* Branson, says she has a *rendezvous*. We have made her comfortable in another room of the hotel. Is it your desire that she join you?

—Kevin, you must think I'm crazy. But I left San Sebastián right after the ceremony and thought I'd make Paris by midnight. I was off by three hours.

I realized she'd been driving half the night. I picked up the phone.

—You must be hungry. And they do brag about room service.

I ordered some onion soup and went to the pantry for a split of champagne.

—Want some?

—Yes, please.

I poured.

—You know, Mercedes, it's okay. There are two beds.

—No! They found me a room on another floor. I'll be fine. I'll have the soup and let you get some sleep.

—Mercedes, a room here is 4,000 Francs. Don't be silly. Stay here. Really. After all, I've been swimming in your pool for years.

—Can I take a hot shower? The car's heater died in Orléans.

—Sure. There's another robe just like this one in the bathroom.

Five minutes later warm zephyrs of Hermès soap insinuated themselves into the suite.

There was a knock on the door. A tuxedo-ed waiter rolled in a table with a tureen of overpowering fragrance and bowls of warm cheese straws, croutons and potato puffs. He lit a candle with a smart flick of his lighter and disappeared.

The shower stopped running.

—God, the smell alone is nourishing.

Mercedes was wrapped in the robe and her auburn hair was wet at the ends. Her eyes were bright as she kissed me lightly. Bundled in the robe like a boxer, she seemed shorter. Of course, she was barefoot. And without make-up she was finer, more pure, just smooth skin, green eyes and pale lips.

I kept her company while she had the soup. We finished the champagne and I went to the pantry for another bottle. It was already four o'clock. I'd get two hours of sleep.

When I came back to the bedroom the lights were out and the candle glowed on a table between the beds.

—I always sleep with a nightlight. Do you mind?

—I guess not. Nightcap?

She held out her glass.

At five o'clock I got into my bed and fell asleep.

Some time later I realized I wasn't alone.

—Please, Kevin. Just let me be here.

She put her hand on my bare chest and her belly against my hip. I lay still, looking at the ceiling. Then she pulled the sheet over us and I was in a tent of Hermès, damp hair, linen and soap.

When her feet slipped under mine, I turned to face her. And she kissed me with cushy lips. Her tongue roamed my mouth with the cold tang of champagne and her breasts pressed against me, full as loaves. Then her hand took my parts and held them, making them heavier. I ran my tongue along her neck, behind her ear, and began to slide down her body sucking kisses as I went. I flattened the shiny cilia around her navel with my tongue and lowered my face to her thighs.

There, I breathed her two natures: the pressed-flower smell of her skin, chaste as plaster dust in church; and the urgent smell below, fresh as a newly-plowed row in a field.

And then I went into her and she was moving her head. And I went into her again. And again.

—*Ahí ... mismo ... sí, ahí ... sí, ¡ay, sí! ¡ay, sí! AY, SÍ.*

When the phone trilled us awake, I grabbed it on the first ring. Mercedes put on her robe and went to open the balcony doors. Cold air came into the room like a possee and I stood with her, looking over the rooftops of Paris in the gray dawn. She rested her head on my shoulder.

I showered with the hottest water I could stand. The shampoo seemed pungent and my stomach was at sea. I rubbed my face with a towel, wishing it were sandpaper.

When I came to the bedroom, Mercedes was on the floor, looking through my suit bag.

—Don't do that. Please don't go through my things.

Her head snapped to look at me and her lip twitched.

She was holding a folded shirt. I took it away. She stood up abruptly.

—Oh, Kevin, I'm sorry. I'm so stupid. I just ... you always look so nice and—she began to cry.

I had twenty minutes to get to my meeting. I took her in my arms.

—Merche ...—I used the tender nickname and kissed her forehead—. Have some breakfast, go swimming, have a massage. Just don't touch my things. I'll be back at ten.

I walked the six blocks to the offices of my cognac client. It was an eighteenth-century townhouse two blocks from the Elysée Palace. I had to report there periodically on the advertising we were doing for them in Spain, which I knew they found trifling. My main contact was an actual count. And he gave me his business card with the royal title each time we met. I had six.

When I got back to the hotel, Mercedes was dressed and packed.

—I ... I haven't touched anything, I swear—she said, earnestly.

I looked at my watch. My flight didn't leave until four.

—Let's go for a walk. I need to buy some things. And if you leave by noon, you'll still make San Sebastián in time for dinner.

—Why don't you come back with me?

—I am not taking a car to Madrid when I can take a ninety-minute flight.

We walked along the Rivoli arcades—everyone's first best stroll in Paris—and I stopped at W.H. Smith to see the new books from the States. We had tea at Angelina's and I window-shopped at Sulka. At Madelaine, we marveled at the Fauchon displays: fruit presented as jewelry.

—I'm going to Ralph Lauren to get some ties.

—Oh, I need some ties, too. For my brothers.

It was past noon when we left the store and I looked across the square at the façade of Lucas Carton.

—Let's have lunch, Mercedes. If you leave Paris at two, you'll still cross into Spain tonight.

In minutes we were ensconced in a crimson *banquette*, watching our creamy reflections in the old mirrors. I wondered if, in its heyday, the *époque* could have been any more *belle* that it was at that very minute.

We had lobster soufflé and the roast duck, with a bottle of Clos de Vougeot. We skipped dessert and had two glasses of *hors d'âge* calvados.

—Kevin—she said, placing a hand on my knee—, I want to go back with you. But I've got my mother's car. I can't leave it in Paris.

—Well ...

—Don't take the plane. How often does one get to Paris? Let's go to Napoleon's tomb. No! Let's go to the Rodin Museum.

—To see what? *The Kiss?*

—Of course! Wait ... what do you see at the Rodin?

—*The Gates of Hell.*

She laughed and smacked my arm good-naturedly. Then, she asked me with Calvados eyes:

—What time do you have to check out of the room?

I cancelled my flight.

We left Paris at five o'clock under rheumy Flemish skies. But an hour later, nearing Chartres, a pastel sunset made it France again and I wanted to see the cathedral. We sat at a café, looking at the façade and I felt Monet and Ruskin with me as the last light kissed the high window.

Mercedes hugged me.

—Oh this is _so_ good.

I scanned a road map while I sipped a *poire*.

—We can overnight in Bordeaux, but I'd rather stay in a place with a name like Périgueux or Bergerac.

She took my hand.

—Kevin, let's not stop. Let's go home, let's sleep in Spain tonight. I've wanted to sleep with you in Spain for three years.

We crossed the border and reached San Sebastián a little after one.

When I got up I called the office and said I'd come in that afternoon. Then I walked from the hotel to the crescent terrace that overlooks the lovely bay of La Concha. The light was egg-y and soft and I watched the long rollers come in from the Atlantic in orderly waves. I sucked in the vibrant air and closed my eyes, listening to the pennants flapping down on the beach.

—Ke-vin! Ke-vin!

Mercedes rushed up to me and I held her close. She had a sweet smell that morning and I breathed it and kissed her hair. Gulls cawed above and a distant cruiser's horn carried in the wind. I felt good; serene and whole.

—Let's have breakfast on the beach.

I bought a local paper and we went down to the shore. There were no swimmers but a hardy wind surfer plowed the ocean in the distance. A few people walked the shoreline, bidding each other good-day, and striped *chaises* were laid out in neat rows on the sand. San Sebastián was the Newport of Spain.

By noon we had left the Basque Country and entered Spain's great orchard—La Rioja. We stopped at the village of Cenicero for *un aperitivo* and a glass of Berberana, the famous red that is their local-boy-made-good. We had a clay pot of braised vegetables: eggplant, artichoke, peppers, carrots and chickpeas cooked slowly in oil and garlic. The flavors were psychedelic.

Back on the road, the fields and vineyards of La Rioja undulated like swaths of fabric: green, garnet and gold. We saw miles of lettuce in Tudela and the red-pepper studded fields of Calahorra.

I wanted to stop for lunch at the medieval castle of Sigüenza. From there, Madrid was an easy three-hour drive. But a few miles away the skies changed. Massive clouds were merging like a rugby scrum and I could see lightning bolts hitting the plain like darts. We parked in front of the castle and made it inside just as the thunderstorm broke and glob-y drops of rain began staining the courtyard.

We had two sherries in the library, glad to be near a fireplace. A maid was lighting the gas lanterns.

Mercedes had been staring at me.

—Kevin, are you happy? I mean in your life, not just at this moment.

I pondered that.

—Well ... I'm very <u>content</u>.

She leaned back in her chair and smiled.

—Well, maybe that's as happy as you get.

We sat at a table by the window, watching the cloud formations move like galleons over the wavy mountain range. I ordered a bottle of Berberana.

—Mercedes, have you called your mother? She might be worried.

—I'll call her from upstairs.

—What's upstairs?

She ran her tongue around the rim of the wineglass.

—Rooms.

We feasted on our bodies, nipping at skin and hair and lips and then we hurried onto each other. I wanted her more than I'd wanted anyone and I took her body and put myself in. And I drove in deep and filled her and her eyes went wide and I pushed and she pleaded and I pushed.

—God, yes! YES! Oh, my beauty! Oh, now! OH! NOW!

And soon I was running down, running down, and spending myself in her.

We pulled away slowly and back onto raft-like pillows and bobbed, gasping and flushed, on the bed. Then she jumped on me and sought my neck and underarms and my thighs and my hot thick part.

Chapter Eight

On a raw October day we all drove to the village of Chinchón to see the last bullfight of the year. It's a medieval town of wood-burning houses in a snail shell pattern above a plaza.

Ramón Cuevas had lived there all his life. It was his turn to host lunch. He said:

—Since it would be unseemly for a young Spanish man to know about cooking, I am hosting three tables on the verandah at Café Iberia. It's a splendid place to see the bullfight.

We toured the village and bought supplies of the local specialties, *anís* and garlic. Every store had pyramids of *anís* bottles in the window and long strands of garlic, like beaded curtains, in the doorway. At three o'clock we went up to our tables. The outdoor seats were sold out and the bullfighters' followers draped the verandahs with banners and bouquets.

—There's something familiar about this—mused Robert Friedlander.

Every seat was filled and people raised their *botas* and tossed carnations into the bullring. The air was cold and alive.

Ramón smiled at Friedlander.

—Well, you have seen this before. And so has each of you.

—I've never been here in my life—argued Cottie.

Randy and I shook our heads in unison. But Mar was smiling.

—This is where the bullfight scene was shot in *Around the World in 80 Days.*

Friedlander smiled with satisfaction.

—Yes. I see it now. Yes.

We ordered braised sausage, stuffed with caraway and fennel and an onion-y salad of tuna belly, olives and eggs, followed by roast suckling pig; leathery on the outside, brimming with yellow broth on the inside.

—You know, guys, I'm not sure about this.

We had finally gotten Barbara to a bullfight and she was having second thoughts.

—Barbara, it's not a sport. But it's not butchery, either,—entreated Mercedes, who loved the bullfight with inherited passion—. It's a spectacle ... a pageant.

—Like the Miss America pageant?—Asked Barbara, timidly.

—Exactly!—Chimed Cottie—. And the bull cries at the end as he's being crowned.

At precisely five o'clock a lone trumpet skewered the air. Three matadors and their entourages entered the ring. People in the stands and balconies hailed their favorites. Mercedes huddled next to me and slipped her hands under my sweater. The sun was going behind the church, and the light was red as cayenne.

Randy and Mar sat close, with a blanket on their knees. Joel stood behind Barbara, kneading the sierra of her shoulders. Cottie and Friedlander opened a bottle of *anís* and Ramón stood on the verandah rubbing his palms, with a Ducados glowing on his lips.

It was a moment both festive and peaceful. We were all well and the late light on our faces was flattering. Ancient chimneys wafted their resinous comfort.

Mercedes kissed my cheek. Her thick hair smelled of smoke, pine and her own rich oils and I held her close. And there we were, doing what we couldn't in America—not just passing the time, but <u>spending</u> the afternoon; dispensing it like currency, <u>allocating</u> it to talk, humor, or contemplation. I suppose we were mimicking the Spaniards' sheer talent for living.

When they brought out the last bull, the sun had gone and it was quite cold. Joel was shivering and coughing. We went to Ramón's house.

Barbara was animated.

—It was thrilling; too bad about the bull, but what can I say?

—Cathartic—said Joel, who looked a little better after sitting by the fire.

Mar waved away their observations.

—No justification is needed. It is the way Spain <u>lives</u>. As much as a mountain or a river, bullfighting is on our map.

Ramón had a two-story house upholstered in books. We sat downstairs sipping homemade *eaux-de-vie* of quince, melon and fig. They somehow combined finesse and power, tasting even riper than the fruits they came from.

—I live here to be grounded in reality. Madrid, and the newspaper, can delude me. But here I am still Ramoncito, the baker's boy.

—Ramón, who do you think will be win the elections?

—Whoever seduces the middle class. And the socialists' courtship of the middle class is bordering on the erotic.

—What about the right-wing candidate?—Asked Cottie.

Ramón snorted derisively.

—What? Is he beneath your contempt?

Ramón thought for a few seconds.

—No, he's right at the level of my contempt.

Back in my office that Monday, a secretary came in with a very long telex.

—If you disregard all the *salutazione* and *arrivederci*, it's brief.

She was a compact *café-au-lait* woman with a crown of reddish corkscrew curls and piercing green eyes. She turned to leave.

—Excuse me, who are you?

—A temp. Your secretary's sick. Or so she says.

She walked out.

My direct line rang. It was Mercedes.

—Don't forget Mar's showing tonight. I'll meet you there at eight. Oh, and I told her we'd buy a painting.

It annoyed me when Mercedes assumed things. The ties she bought in Paris for her "brothers" were foisted on me and she was churlish when I wouldn't wear them.

—No, Mercedes, we will not buy a painting. You or I may buy a painting, to hang in your house or mine. But we are not we.

—Oh, Kevin, don't be disagreeable—she said, and hung up.

I liked Mar's work; her palette was like Sorolla's, my favorite Spanish painter. But she didn't paint luminous scenes of bathers on sun-splashed beaches; she did portraits *à la* Lucien Freud. She'd done a great likeness of Randy and had asked me to sit, but I didn't think I had the patience.

The scene at the gallery was typical: a loud mob eating, drinking and smoking in a room that was hung with art but, for their purposes, might as well be hung with hams.

Joel waved over weakly, looking ache-y and wan. I began to 'walk the room', spending the requisite minute before each portrait. And I was surprised by a likeness of Queen Sofía.

—You know,—said a voice at my side—The Queen herself posed for it. Mar's mother is a dame at court.

He was a handsome, brilliantined man I'd seen in popular magazines. He smiled, like the shuffle of a deck of cards.

—I am Carlos de la Concha y Carbajal—we shook hands—. And if you are thinking of buying this painting, then I'm afraid we are rivals. Ah, there's the artist. Please excuse me.

He glided toward Mar.

I continued my dutiful tour of the show until suddenly, I was staring at a portrait of Mercedes.

—Surprise!—Mercedes herself was standing behind me.

—When did you sit for her?

—Last month, when you went to Italy.

It was a true likeness, girlish and vulnerable.

—See, Kevin? See why I said we'd buy a painting?

—I don't know, Mercedes ... it's the kind of thing ... don't you think your mother would want it?

She was dumbstruck and I could see I'd said the wrong thing.

—My mother?!?

She stormed off through the crowd and I decided not to follow.

The next morning at work I found out my regular secretary had hepatitis and would be out for weeks. I called in the temp I'd seen the day before.

—I'm sorry, I don't know your name.

—Sonia.

She was small, but full-figured. And rounded, but not soft. Her face was strong and there was something un-Spanish to it.

—Sonia, please send a messenger to the Prado Museum to get two tickets. The Italians from FIAT are here and I want to invite them.

—Everyone goes to the Prado,—she said, with a sniff.

—Well ... yes. It's a great museum.

—It's bourgeois. Except for Goya's black paintings.

It was an impertinent remark, but I couldn't ignore it.

—Any museum you <u>do</u> like?

—The nineteenth-century collection at the Casón. Where they put the Guernica.

—The Guernica was at MOMA in New York all my life. I've seen it.

—Go past it, to the first gallery, and see the historical murals. Then go upstairs and see the Fortunys and Madrazos. She turned to leave.

—Wait ... if I go on my own, I might ... miss something—I was staring at her and she stared back—. Why don't you come along and explain it to me?

She tilted her head and said, slowly:

—See you there at six.

Picasso's Guernica, at the entrance to the museum, was assaultive as ever. But Sonia walked right past it into the first gallery. It's a huge, hushed room with banquettes and four vast works: *The Death by Firing Squad of General Torrijo, Juana La Loca, The Lovers of Teruel*, and *The Expulsion of the Jews*. The sweeping, gloriously flawed history of Spain was on those wall-length canvases; moments when Spaniards brought woes of biblical dimension upon themselves. It was all there, the regal setting hinting at rot, the ominous event no one seems able to stop. And also, from the plains of Castille to the cliffs of Galicia, the supremely pitiless landscape.

Upstairs, as though emerging from a cave into light, I saw Fortuny's butterfly-kiss brushstrokes of Oriental salons and comely Gypsies. But, best of all, I met the full-blooded women of Madrazo, the actresses and courtesans of that gay century; amused, wise, and achingly beckoning.

Sonia had stood back to let me observe, occasionally murmuring a bit of salt about the painter or the model, but letting me absorb the full impact of those all-knowing Bovarys caught on canvas.

We saw only two rooms in the museum, but took two hours to do it. I was spent. And I had not seen another visitor. But then, who had ever heard of this place?

—Spain stopped collecting when she stopped having kings. And our best modern artists, Picasso, Miró and Dalí, disdained the regimes that came after. In fact, Franco was so philistine, that we have no twentieth-century Spanish collection. The smallest Picasso museum anywhere dwarfs anything here.

We were in La Fídula, a classical-music café on Huertas.

—Sonia, what's your last name?

—Mondragón.

—That's Basque.

—My father is from Bilbao.

—And where in Madrid do you live?

She sipped her drink and smiled.

—Nowhere you or your friends have ever seen. It's a short street called Libertad, in the old part of the city.

—Of course I know it. That's where Bocaíto is.

She arched an eyebrow, impressed.

—You know, I've been with you for three hours and you haven't had a cigarette. Are you the only woman in Madrid who doesn't smoke?

She smiled.

—I have no small vices.

The next day I had lunch with Cottie.

—Kevin! What are you thinking? You're the boss. You can't go out with your secretary.

—She's not my secretary. She's a temp.

—Even worse! The Gringo going out with the hourly help. Kevin, you'll lose face at the office.

—I don't know, Cottie. She's just so ... unusual.

—Kevin, what about Mercedes?

—We haven't spoken since the night at the gallery. Technically, we're not seeing each other now. So that means ...

—It means you call the temp agency, and say you want an old, militant lesbian.

—Cottie, it's so complex. There's culture there, without pretension. Smarts ... irreverence; a fresh eye for things. And ... fun.

—You just described *me*!

—Well, there's ... the physical thing—I said.

—Oh, that.

—She's ... exotic.

—Whoa, Kevin.—Cottie began singing a song from the '70s.

—*And the sailors say: Brandy, you're a fine girl.*

—Come on, Cottie.

—Look, Kevin, we all want something, a prize of some kind. And that's great. But this girl is no prize.

—Oh? How would you know? What's your prize?

Cottie took a breath and looked straight at me.

—A novel. I'm writing a novel.

—I thought so. I saw two poems in a London magazine.

He shook his head.—Practice swings. I'm working on the novel full-time.

—What's it about?

He looked in my eyes.—It's about wishing I wrote like Fitzgerald.

—And ...?

—Well, I do write like Fitzgerald, when he was twelve.

—What's the title?

—*The Same Love Twice.*

—Sounds like Scott to me.

—Now I need 400 pages just like the title.

—Got an ending?

—Nope. But I promise you it will be trenchant. All books now are *trenchant.*

—Why are you writing here? Why Spain?

—Climate's good, women are fine, wine's cheap. And something about Spain sure bailed out Hemingway and Graves and Irving.

—Washington Irving?

—No, you idiot, Clifford Irving.

—And excuse me for asking, but how do you survive in the meantime?

—I was Granny's favorite. And she bought Xerox at six; 50,000 shares.

The two hot discos in Madrid opened at one-thirty in the morning and we'd go after dinner. Joy was the 'young' place and Pachá was for those who had jobs. Spanish men like to stroll up to the gate at Pachá and hurl their car keys at the valet. This gave them the momentum to slip past the bouncer—the powerful, inscrutable Martín. Sometimes it worked. And, sometimes, an imperceptible signal alerted the woman inside to stop you and ask for the cover charge.

I liked getting to Pachá for the opening set. That year the deejay always started with Kool and the Gang's *Fresh*, I got my vodka *limón* just as the silky song strobed over the dance floor.

> —*Conversation's been goin' round,*
> *people talkin' 'bout the girl who's*
> *come to town ...*

Barbara Isaacs slid onto the dance floor. She was a regular. Rumor had it she even got mail at Pachá. I did know she kept a raincoat and boots there.

—Hey, Barbara. How was Portugal?

—Same. Lisbon's sad. It looks ... unraveled.

Barbara, like Cottie, had to cross the border into Portugal or France every six months to get her passport stamped and be able to come back to Spain for another six months. She went to Portugal because it was closer, and cheaper, than France. People who didn't have a full-time employer did this all the time.

—Hey, Kevin, have you seen Joel? There's no answer at his place.

—Nope. I was going to ask you.

We swayed to the lilting music.

—How's the stringer-work?

—Okay. I got a piece in Cosmo and two photos in Glamour.

—Mercedes sees your byline all the time.

—Which brings me: Where is she? I heard things.

I shrugged and did a couple of turns to the chorus.

—Kevin, that girl is nuts about you. Believe me, women can tell.

—Barbara, I met someone.

She stopped dancing and gaped at me.

—Kevin, you can't. A girl like Mercedes ... that's life without parole.

At three A.M. the first set climaxed with *Everybody Wants To Rule the World*. It was rinsing in my ears when I slipped out, panting and damp, to head for the line of taxis.

—Pachá? That's a place for preppy drunks who can't dance.

—I'll dispute a third of that. I <u>can</u> dance.

Sonia and I were at Bar Hispano having a drink after work.

—One night I'll really take you dancing. To a place called Ola-Ola. Brazilian music.

—Now that you mention Brazil ... do you have any family there?

—No, why?

—It's just that you look ...

—Darker.

—I was going to say «exotic».

—No, I'm not Brazilian and I don't have any Gypsy blood. My mother, though, was Cuban. And she may have been a *mulata*. She died when I was little.

—Excuse me, are you Kevin Byrne?—Asked the waiter—. Telephone.

It was Barbara.

—Thank God I found you. You gotta come to Joel's place now. Please.

Ten minutes later Sonia and I were climbing up the four flights of stairs to Joel's attic on Berenjena Street. Barbara and Cottie were waiting for us.

—Now, Kevin, when you go in, act normally.

It was a small place, but tastefully done; shiny pine floors, forest-green walls, black leather chairs. On the walls were lithographs of Greek Olympians, runners and wrestlers, and splashy color photos of Australian lifeguards. And cookbooks, maybe 100 of them, in a floor-to-ceiling case.

Joel was in bed. He smiled self-consciously when he saw me. He was sucking on a plastic tube from a machine that whirred by his side. He looked faded. He held up a palm, asking me to wait. I sat on the edge of the bed. Two minutes later he took the tube out of his mouth and turned off the machine.

—It's a (*cough*) ... nebulizer. I need it four times a day. My lungs are kinda clogged.

I knew at once and he could tell.

—But it's not what you think. Well, it <u>is</u> what you think, but it's complicated by the weather, so it looks worse than it is. Just have to get over the flu. Get stronger. So I can get back to work.

—Joel, have you told your parents?

—No. The only person in the States who knows is Simone. I wrote her last week. I mean if, God forbid, something happens, I'd like someone I know to go see them. My father's 73.

He began coughing and didn't seem able to stop.

Barbara wiped his eyes and mouth with tissues.

—You know, I'm going to get better and then go back home. Spanish food in New York is still *paella-sangría-flan*. They don't know from *tapas* ... I could be the *tapas* messiah.

Then he started coughing again. Out on the stairwell Barbara said:

—It looks pretty bad. He's going to a state clinic but his Spanish social security won't cover any special medication. I think he should go back to the States.

—Are his parents religious?—I asked.

—They will be when they find out.

Later, we sat glumly in La Fídula. Occasionally, someone would mention third-hand hearsay about some miraculous remission. Sonia shook her head.

—We've had this in Spain for five years. Famous, rich people go to Houston or Zurich, have whole-body transfusions. Hopeless. And it's a cruel disease. The person feels better one day and there's euphoria. Then comes the relapse.

—The first case I ever saw—recalled Cottie—was an editor at Random House. I'd taken him my first stories from Dartmouth, awful stuff. And this guy looked like an El Greco, with tubes going into his nose. And he was still working! I'll never forget, he hands back the stories, looks me in the eyes, and says:

—You want to be a writer? Go out there and <u>live</u>.

—Six weeks later, he was dead—said Cottie.

When I got home there was a registered letter from Mercedes. She had called me at work, but I hadn't spoken to her. I felt pretty guilty about that. But I didn't want to open the letter, either.

Chapter Nine

That Saturday I skipped the lunch at Barbara's to be with Sonia. Until then, I'd only seen her on weekdays. She met me in front of the Army Museum.

—Ever been inside?—She asked, cocking her head.

—No, the word *Army* has connotations for an American.

—Let me show it to you.

It was all there: the Armada's sea battles re-enacted in glass cases, the captured flags of the African campaigns, the gleaming portraits of the Hell's Angels *conquistadores*. But the best exhibit had three vehicles: an open carriage, a 1930's limo, and a '73 Dodge, in single file.

—This is the carriage Alfonso XIII rode in on his wedding day. Those brown stains are his blood. He survived. The limo with the Bonnie-and-Clyde holes is where General Prim was assassinated. And this scrunched up heap is where Franco's successor was riding when he was blown up by Basque terrorists.

—The Spanish flag is yellow and red, Kevin. Sun and blood.

She wanted to buy me lunch and I protested patronizingly. She took me to a small, hidden café.

The owner-waiter-chef was a large and brooding man. There was no menu.

—So how do you order?

—Abraham keeps bringing out things. You tell him when to stop.

A platter appeared with a large vine leaf on which the word 'prologue' was scripted in mayonnaise.

Then came pumpkin soup, in an actual pumpkin, a partridge mousse shaped like a bird in flight, then a 'chessboard' with alternating squares of smoked salmon and eel. The 'pieces' were carved from, carrots. I snapped the crown off my 'queen'. A loin of pork had pork-rind ears and tail and the vegetable platter was actually an artist's palette made from a chickpea pita and the pigments were purees of red, yellow, and green peppers. The 'brush' poking through the hole was a long bread stick with fried vermicelli 'bristles'.

—It's all exquisite. And the wines.

—Small vineyards with no budget for labels or marketing. Guess that's hypocritical since I'm being paid by an ad agency.

—No, Sonia, a lot of what we do is artifice. But this food …

—It's called simplicity. Abraham has a lousy location and zero charisma. He can't charge what other restaurants do. And he gets the most out of the cheapest raw materials. Have you ever had lentils, Kevin?

—No.

—Well, they're a ten *pesetas* delicacy.

Abraham brought out complimentary thimbles of home-made liqueur, cold as liquid nitrogen, and the check, with Sonia promptly took.

—He's scary.

—Maybe. But Basque men can cook.

I didn't know quite how to take that.

In a dank part of Madrid is a maze of streets with names like *Remorse* and *Have Mercy*. In its midst is *Libertad*, where Sonia lived in a fourth floor walk-up. The living room was lime green, the floors were yellow. On a red wooden table, a sunflower graced a wine jug and two Frida Kahlo prints were on the wall. The tiny kitchen could barely hold two and the bathroom was more like a phone booth. The bedroom was indigo and white, with a hemp-like carpet on the floor.

—That's sisal, from the Philippines. Take your shoes off and walk on it; therapeutic.

I did.—It's like walking on a large Triscuit.

On the dresser were a coiled wooden rosary and a photo of a couple next to a cannon on the wall of a Spanish fort.

—My parents at Morro Castle in Cuba. Do you want some cold *anís*? It's all I have.

—Sure. I went to the kitchen.

—No, I don't have a fridge. All the cold things are on the window ledge.

I opened the window. There, forty feet above the sidewalk were bottles of milk and *anís*, and anonymous bundles. I heard a guitar-y lament behind me.

—Portuguese music, called *fado*. It's good in the afternoon. Just don't listen to it at three in the morning. I'll get glasses. Make yourself comfortable.

The sofa was old and sapphire blue.

—It's from the lobby of an old movie theater that closed last year. And my 'coffee table' is a giant drum that used to hang above a toy store that went broke. So there's a lot of bad commercial karma here. But it's only 40,000 pesetas a month. We're comfortable.

—We? Who are <u>we</u>?

—My brother Pablo lives with me. He's in a band.

—Sonia, why do you work through an agency? They take half of what we pay you.

—Look at the street sign on the corner, *Libertad*. I want to be able to <u>not</u> work the days I feel like it.

The record had finished. She leaned down over the victrola to change it.

—What would you like to hear?

I was seeing her from the back: her undulant shape and the rope-like hair.

—Honestly? The sunset glared into the room, soaking it in a paprika-red light.

—I'd like to hear <u>you</u> ... talk, sing ...

She laughed.

—Be careful what you wish for.

She emptied the *anís* bottle into my glass.

—Sonia ...

—I have an idea. This light is very good. Pull down the blinds.

I did. A hard slatted light seared through the jalousies.

—I think I'd like to take your picture like that, Kevin, striped like a tiger.

—Um ... okay.

She came back into the room with an old Pentax. She brought it up to her eye, held it, then brought it down.

—No, it doesn't work with your sweater. It's better on bare skin. Why don't you take it off while I change the record?

She put on an album of Ryuiichi, the Japanese performance artist.

—Better?—I asked.

She was adjusting the light meter.

—Stand by the sunflower.

The light came through the slatted blinds like swords, painting my skin.

Again she brought the camera up to her eye and prepared to shoot.

—No. The pants. Those corduroys just fight the horizontal stripes from the window. Are you wearing underwear?

—Of course.—What was this woman thinking?

The syncopated music chopped into the room.

—Strip down. Let's see.

I slid out of my pants.

—Oh, no, boxer shorts. You won't look like a tiger in those. I'm sorry, you have to lose the shorts.

—Um … I'm not sure about this.

My heart was drumming. And the music seemed even louder and I'd had too much *anís*.

—I know. You can wear my underwear.

—What??

—Wear my thong.

—I don't …

—Yes. Nudity is not the point. You're a tiger. So I don't want the nudity to distract. My thong is the simplest thing.

She began to undress. She slipped off the sweater. She wore nothing underneath and her breasts jutted out like brown dirigibles. Then she shook out of her skirt. She wore a black satin triangle in front and a string, like a black noodle, up the back. She snapped it off.

—Put this on.

—Sonia … I don't know.

She came over and pulled down my underwear.

—Put on my thong.

I did it quickly. The black patch hardly covered me and the string in the back was still warm. The music was deafening.

She began taking pictures.

—Face the light. Show me your profile. Head up now. There. Don't move.—She snapped six shots in a row. Then, still looking at me, though not *at* me, but at a form, she tossed the camera onto the sofa—. Those will be good.

I didn't know whether to change back into my clothes and my discomfiture must have showed.

She smiled and walked over to me.

—Now, I'm going to put on your shorts ... there. Hah! It's ... kind of arousing. Oh, this is like phantom-limb syndrome; I actually feel a member or something, swelling under the shorts. Come here, touch me here, as though you were trying to arouse a man, to make him hard. Go on, Kevin.

—Sonia, I don't think ...

—Kevin, just do it. Make like you're stroking me, like a man, and I will touch you like I would touch a woman.

—Sonia, this is ...

She slipped off the thong and I let her caress me, at the front and in the back. And I closed my eyes.

—Be a girl for me and you'll see how good you feel ... oh Kevin ... let go. You've been living with the emergency brake on your feelings.

A little before midnight Sonia walked me to the corner. She didn't have a phone and I wanted to call Barbara.

—Hi. Sorry I missed the lunch.

—Kevin! Lunch, schmunch; where have you been? Mercedes was here. She cried for an hour. And Randy showed up drunk, 'cause he saw Mar with that Carlos-de-whatever guy. So he had a fight, with himself, in my living room. It looks like Nagasaki. Then he stormed out to look for her. I'm <u>worried</u>.

My head was pounding. I called Cottie.

—Guess where I was tonight, Coach? Jail!

—What have you done?

—Nothing! I was visiting young Randall, who found Mar with her Marquis and beat them both up. Does your agency have a lawyer?

—Yeah, but he does contract law. Might recommend someone, though. Still, Randy shouldn't spend the night in a Madrid jail.

—Can't help him, *Monsignor*. It's large bail and banks don't open 'til Monday.

Later at Sonia's with incense and tea, she made an observation.

—Your friend Randy-he's a tall blond American with a swimmer's body. And every upper-class Spanish girl wants one of those for her charm bracelet. But, in the long run, a girl like Mar Martínez Aleya wants Carlos de la Concha y Carbajal. That is her destiny.

That year I ran with a group of expats called the Harriers, mostly embassy people. Each Sunday one of us would set a run on a natural trail within an hour's drive from Madrid.

That morning the run was in Colmenar, donkey-colored country full of darting hares and wildcats. It was sunny, with dew steaming off the bushes of rosemary and gorse. I enjoyed the scrabbliness of the run and the two freezing creeks I'd had to ford. Afterwards, a man who always seemed to finish around the same time, came over to me, while I sucked on a beer.

—Hi. Bill Ellis.

He was ruddy, about 50, with a salt and pepper crew-cut and the hand-shake of a blacksmith.

—You know, Kevin, Nancy Kroll from Commercial Section told me about you.

—Ah, the California olive lady. What section are you in?

—Let's just say I roam. Freelancer, they'd say in your line of work. He laughed.

The beer suddenly felt glacial going down. That laugh could only be described as *hearty* which I always thought meant *false*.

—You know, Kevin, I understand you speak a few languages. And that you've really become integrated in Spain. Almost a local.

—Who said that?—I asked, pleasantly.

—Nancy.

—You know, Bill, I've got to go.

He smiled.

—Sure. But take my card. If you ever want to do something interesting with those languages, give me a call.

It was an embassy card, with a phone number, but no name.

That night Sonia took me to Ola-Ola, a Brazilian haunt three stories below street level. Music bounced off the walls, which seemed to shine with the steam from the dancer's bodies. And this was not casual swaying, this was extreme dancing.

—You know—I yelled above the din—, It would be hard to run up those three flights of stairs if you wanted to bolt.

—That's the idea.

Then a caramel-colored boy, about sixteen, came up to Sonia. They kissed on the mouth.

—Kevin, this is my brother Pablo.

We shook hands. He was wiry, with precise movements, and his sister's green grape eyes.

—Sonia, I need 2,000 *pesetas*. I'm going to the movie marathon at Ideal.

Sonia's face went rigid.

—Pablo, the marathon costs 100 *pesetas*. Why do you need 2,000?

He glanced away impatiently.

—Come on, Sonia. I might want to eat something later.

In the corner, I could see a tall African with shades looking at us. Sonia quickly pulled two thousand-peseta notes from her pocket and pushed them at him.

—Okay. Then I'm going to the marathon, too. And I want to see you there. Understand?

He kissed her quickly and slipped off.

—Anything wrong?—I asked when we got outside.

—Big sister stuff. But don't worry.

Later, waiting in line for tickets, she brightened.

—You'll like this. It's the most decrepit movie house in Europe. They can't afford first-run films so they have these all-night genre marathons with old prints, lousy sound and piss-soaked seats. It's great.

It was two in the morning and the place was already thronged with Madrid's unique fauna.

—We're just in time. By three o'clock there aren't any tickets left.

The cavernous cinema was gamy and dank, and the mossy clientele contributed to the ether.

—The best things tonight are two music videos about vampires and werewolves in Paris. The movies suck.

We stayed until dawn. Occasionally Sonia would get up and scan the seats. She never saw her brother.

On Monday I finally called Mercedes. We met at Bar Independencia. It was cold but sunny and we sat outside. The chestnut trees were wet and scuffed, with a few unfelled yellow leaves gleaming like vinyl.

—Mercedes, I'm really sorry about this.

—About what? Not taking my calls? Not answering my letters? Or about cheating on me with a Cuban slut?

She was wearing make-up and lipstick, which she'd never done.

—Mercedes, I'm not cheating on you; we're not married or engaged or living ...

—We are a couple! Ask any of our friends!

—Mercedes ... they don't decide these things.

—I don't care! You've got to ... just snap out of it!

She stared at me with urgent eyes and her small fists were trembling at her side. I looked at her.

—I don't think I can—I admitted.

Her eyes widened with umbrage.

—Well, do you <u>want</u> to snap out of it?

—No—I said, eventually.

One of her tears, salty and hot, sprang onto my lip. And she began to shake. I leaned over to hold her. She pushed back to look in my eyes.

—Kevin, please! Let's fix this! We can fix this!

—No, we can't, Merche—I said, my voice breaking—. Nobody can.

That afternoon, I called Cottie.

—Did you spring Randy?

—Oh, yeah. Cost 250,000 pesetas. But that's not the problem, Mahatma. He's up on battery and both these people are like local royalty. The marquis guy is like the national mascot. Randy could get three years.

There was a cabinet in my office full of cognac bottles, presents from production houses, printers and the like. I'd never opened any of them. Instead, I would re-wrap one or two whenever I needed to give a gift; ideally not back to the same printers and producers. I opened a bottle of the gorgeous Lepanto and poured half a glass. At my desk, I made a call.

—Ellis.

—Hi. Kevin Byrne. We met on the run yesterday.

—What can I do for you, Kevin?

—Well, a friend, an American is in legal trouble. I thought ...
—What kind of trouble, son?
He sounded as patronizing as a high-school guidance counselor.
—I thought maybe the embassy ...
—Let me have the facts, son.

Chapter Ten

I don't know why we decided to make Thanksgiving dinner that year; we'd never celebrated in Madrid before. As an American ritual, it was largely unknown, as were the ingredients for the meal. But I think we sought refuge in something familiar.

Nancy Kroll, Cottie's embassy mole/girlfriend, had bought a Butterball turkey at the airbase. An Air Force transport had also brought fresh corn, cranberries and yams, plus mince and pumpkin pies—all of which found their way to our table. Barbara and I thought we could fill in the blanks from things available in Spain. In fact, the stuffing (some of us called it 'dressing', a slight polemic) was made from day-old Spanish rye, *chorizo*, oysters, chestnuts, partridge livers and gizzards, and raisins soaked in sherry. It was wonderful. We even made a velvety clam chowder and a great three bean salad, all with local ingredients.

What we couldn't buy, however, even at the air base, were the forests of New England; or the same smells coming from every neighbor's doorway in a Manhattan highrise; or the looks on faces leaving mass that day in Savannah or Saratoga. None of that made it onto the C-130 transport.

We made the dinner at Joel's place. He was too sick to go out by then, though he coached us from the bedroom while Barbara and I worked in the kitchen. Some of the others had taken a break to join us: Piet and his boyfriend, Friedlander and Ramón. It was awkward, though no one said so, not to see Mercedes or Mar. But the remarkable thing was having Randy there in the first place, though this was also going be his farewell dinner. After I called Bill Ellis, Randy's case was mysteriously dropped. But the price for this legerdemain (and the outcry among the Madrid aristocracy) was an extradition agreement brokered by the embassy: Randy would have to leave Spain that Saturday.

—Talk about having things to be grateful for—said Randy, nursing a beer—. And I owe you my life, Kevin. I couldn't have done time here.

When you get back to the States—he said, lifting his drink and looking at me—, you name it, Man.

I smiled weakly, trying not to think of Ellis, someday calling in this very big marker.

The meal was mnemonic. The moist, woodsy turkey reminded Cottie of long walks on the leaf-covered grounds of his Rhode Island home—in his favorite sweater and his L.L.Bean boots. Barbara and Joel laughed together remembering their mothers, tentatively following the WASP-y rite, and making the stuffing with matzah. It had been different in California, though. Randy alleged having always had avocado salad and kiwi pie with his turkey.

I remembered a distant Thanksgiving, before going away to Lawrenceville, while my parents were still alive. But I didn't remember the meal; only asking permission to leave the table, and then playing touch football with some kids in Washington Square Park, throwing the ball as hard as I could in the gloom, hoping I'd hear somebody catch it.

We began our dinner late on purpose, because of the six-hour time difference. Most of our families and friends in the States sat down around eight P.M. Madrid time, and so did we. Two hours later, Sonia was making coffee, Cottie and Randy called their parents. Barbara spoke to her father and also to Joel's. Joel got on briefly before running out of breath. I was thinking about people I might want to talk to, when the doorbell rang.

Piet opened the door. It was Simone Du Lac.

—Surprise, Guys! I've been looking everywhere for you.—She saw the spread on the table—. Wow! And you're doing the Thanksgiving thing; that's great!

She took off her fur coat and went around the room, switch-kissing everyone until she turned to Joel, propped up on the couch, smiling. She extended her long arms to him and I thought dreadfully she might actually expect him to come to her. But she went over and took his small body in her arms. And I thought it was a pretty tender moment.

—I'm in town scouting locations for a New York director. I'm staying at the Palace, but I wanted to see all of you. By the way, can I help myself to some of that? I didn't eat on the plane. Even though it's business class, the food's still awful.

We all sat down again and watched her eat with gusto. She talked about how vibrant New York was just then, and the well-known people she had met or worked with.

—You people; let me just take a sip—hmmmmm—, you people have to go back. Hell, most of you are from there. And you Piet, Friedlander, everything fresh being done in your fields is being done there. And the '80s are just so much New York's <u>moment</u>!

We listened, kind of blankly, to tales of home, being told by a stranger.

Later, alone with her in Joel's kitchen, she asked how I was.

—I mean, really, Kevin.

—I'm fine.—I said, as earnestly as possible.

She smiled puckishly.

—And is that smouldery one out there yours? That must keep you awake ... nights.

I left around midnight. I had an early meeting the next day. Out in the street, the nude trees combed the wind until it whistled. It had gotten very cold. I put my hands in my pockets and tried to retract my head into my coat. Just as I got to my building and was hurriedly opening the doors, a fresh gust blew by me and I looked back toward the park. I took a deep breath of the night and got that first metallic whiff of snow.

WINTER
(One Year Later)

Chapter Eleven

—I'm not going back to New York until I've published my novel—said Cottie, addressing his wineglass.

—I'll go back when I get my name on a line of clothes, period—affirmed Barbara looking up at the ceiling from the couch.

—What about you, Kevin?—Asked Ramón.

—Well, I'd like to go back for the World Series.

—Kevin, we're talking about going back to <u>live</u>—said Cottie.

It was that leaden hour when it's too early for dinner and too late for a siesta.

—I don't know that I want to do that—I said, eventually.

—Whadd'ya mean?—Barbara sprang from the couch like a jack-in-the-box.

—I mean that Spain may be home for the foreseeable … whatever.

Barbara and Cottie looked at me as though I'd announced an imminent sex change.

Robert Friedlander offered support.

—I quite understand. Spain is alluring.

Ramón weighed in.

—And Americans become especially besotted. You are simultaneously the world's least worldly people, and the most adventurous. You either refuse to learn the language or you apply for citizenship.

—Ant—added Piet as he stroked Pan and Vino, at his feet like ottomans—, there huff neffer bin any German or Dutch or British bullfighters. But der huff bin two American matadors: John Fulton ant Sidney Franklin.

—And Franklin was from Brooklyn!—Exclaimed Cottie—. A Dodger fan, a bagel baby!

Sonia came in from her kitchen with tea.

—Sounds like the Americans are homesick. Why don't you go home to visit? You're not exiles. And no law says you must be a success before you can show your face; it's not a college reunion.

—Sonia, you don't get it. The three of us hit a speed bump in New York—said Barbara, patiently—. Jeez, we were on the side of the road. And if we want to get back in the New York lane of life …

—Kill that metaphor, pleeeze!—Begged Cottie.

—Barbara has a point—Robert said—. I wasn't getting any work in London. If I manage to get back in the business there, it will be on the strength of what I do here.

—I'm taking pictures next week for Spanish Vogue—Piet added—. In Holland I vass taking bets.

Sonia shook her head.

—You are confusing your little success fantasies with the idea of home, of where you're from. Of the places that made you. Are you telling me you won't go back to New York until you can appear there as Fashion-Designer Barbie and Novelist Ken? Kevin, Cottie, Barbara, you want to be there. Christmas is three weeks away. Aren't you thinking of that tree where the people skate? Or the windows on the Fifth Avenue?—She looked at her watch and smiled—. It's now lunchtime in Manhattan. Martini time. And don't tell me the three of you can't afford the plane fare.

Cottie looked abstractedly as Vino lapped at his glass.

—Young lady might have a point—he said, softly.

—If there are still any seats left—said Barbara—. Probably no seats left.

Sonia saw something out the window and turned to me with a wry smile.—It's snowing outside. Imagine it snowing on the Central Park.

We all went out into the flinty afternoon. The snow was falling thick and wet, sticking to the street like coconut ice. And I couldn't help thinking of New York in snow, standing in the park with the 360-degree view of those Hopper buildings and their O'Keefe plumes of steam. The Plaza. The Dakota.

I turned to Sonia.

—Would you come with me?

—I can't, Kevin.

—Why not? You've never been.

—I can't leave Pablo. I don't dare.

—But why?

She looked down at the quilted sidewalk.

—Drugs. I'm afraid if I leave him for just one night, he'll wake up dead. I need to go back. Pablo should be home soon.

We all said good-by and I walked home with my dogs. By the time I got there they had small mounds of snow on their backs and looked like pack animals. The front doors of my building had two brass knockers shaped like hands in prayer. For whatever reason, I took the dogs upstairs and went back into the street and toward the church of Los Jerónimos on the corner.

I had concluded years earlier that I was an a-la-carte Catholic; selective, lazy. For Lent I would give up things that I didn't particularly crave, like cognac or something. And though I did have *faith*, I was really just a New-Testament person after all. Still, that evening I felt the need to pray, though I wasn't sure what for.

Once Cottie, Barbara and I bought tickets, Friedlander, Piet and Ramón signed up, too. I booked rooms at the old Mayfair on 65th and Park and made arrangements for a van to meet us at JFK. Because I'd been so busy planning the trip and making sure I was all caught up at work, I hadn't really thought about being back in the States. Until I was on the plane.

That's when I saw the tall kids returning from their semesters at Salamanca, clutching their guitars and bullfight posters. And the embassy families and the local heads of Procter and Gamble and General Foods España, heading back to Rye and Roanoke and Redondo Beach. A black steward handed me a blanket and said:—gets cold up there, mah man. Then a crinkly-eyed, white-haired stewardess asked me to retrieve a tiny bottle of vodka that had rolled under my seat.

—Sweetie, can you get that rascal for me?

That's when it hit me. I was already in the States. That TWA 747 sitting on the runway in Madrid, being loaded with Samsonites and back-packs and hundreds of trays of turkey and sweet potatoes was already part of the United States. So were the crew and the Bing Crosby song playing in the cabin. But, most of all, it was the captain's voice right before take-off that told me I was already in the U.S.

—Lazengemmun, Cap'n King here. Once I get
the go I'll take 'er up to, oh, 35,000
feet or so. An' you'll be able to sit back,
have a drink. I'll get back to you once we're
over the water. Meantime, I wanna wish you all
a merry Christmas. I'm proud to be takin'
you home.

That voice! California's sequoias were in that voice, along with all the maple syrup in Vermont. In that voice were all the men who march on Veteran's Day, the choir in Saint Patrick's and the crowd at Lambeau Field. That voice had the sturdiness of a Texas derrick and the softness of a Pennsylvania quilt. And that's why I felt, even looking out the window at the wet gray tarmac, I was already home.

The TWA flight landed in New York City just in time for dinner.

—Lady, you want I take FDR Drive?—Asked our Iranian driver.

—Second Avenue's nicer.

—Lodda conzdrogshon now, Lady. More subway. We take better FDR.

—Then why did he ask?—Muttered Barbara.

The December night was velvet behind the skyline's tiara. I'd been back twice in three years, but just for quick business meetings; number-crunching confabs in anonymous rooms. And both times in August. That wasn't New York. New York was landing at JFK with the smell of runway rubber and jet fuel and the cold slapping you in the face when you stepped outside. New York was the black skycap chewing his White Owl as he brought your bags to the curb.

—Is that twelve dollars for all the bags?—I asked.

—Dass bof' ends, an' the middle, too, Boss—New York was this.

Driving on the bridge, the midtown skyscrapers stacked into view.

—You know—mused Cottie—, I haven't seen that in four years. And it sure is goddamned jewel-y.

—Is that the Empire State Building?—Asked Friedlander—. Why is it lit up red and green?

—For Christmas—I said—. And if the Yankees win the World Series, it's blue and white. Orange at Halloween.

Piet smiled and shook his head.

—America ... dat's vunderfull.

—You know—said Ramón—, I have seen that view in many photos and in those sentimental Woody Allen films. But it's still breathtaking in real life. The sheer power ... the <u>means</u> you people have to do such things. I will tell you: if the Japanese had seen this view, they would not have bombed Pearl Harbor. He took out a cigarette and flicked his lighter.

—No smoking here!—Cried the driver, staring irately in the rear-view mirror—. Where you think you are?

—Whadd'ya mean, there's no listing?

Barbara was in my hotel room trying to book a table. She asked the operator for Beau Village, Casey's and Granados, all the old standbys. No listings.

—Let's walk over to Moon's—I said—. It's only six blocks. C'mon, think of the venison.

Out on Park Avenue, we meandered, looking up at everything. The night was freezing and we were beat from the trip, but it was invigorating just to be back. Back in the Big A. We were going to Moon's, a quirky uptown *boite* run by an eye-patched ex-broker with that nickname who cooked up things like boar and ostrich. But when we got there the place was dark and the shingle was gone. On the door was a new plaque: David Rothenberg, D.D.S

—Eclipsed—quipped Cottie.

We ended up at Tavern on the Green, a place we had prided ourselves on never having visited. But it was 11:30 and there were six of us and they had a table. We sat in the famous tourist den, feeling a bit sheepish. The waiter didn't help.

—Well, Folks, I hope you're finding New York as friendly as ... Michigan? Or is it Minnesota? Help me out here.

Afterwards at the hotel bar we had several expensive Spanish brandies.

Barbara called out to Ramón.

—Hey, Minnesota Slim! Help me out here!

—Brethren, if we look like we're from Minnesota, we've really lost our fastball—Cottie said.

The next morning we went on separate pilgrimages. Barbara took the subway up to the Bronx to see Joel's parents. He'd died in New York from AIDS almost a year earlier. Cottie flew up to Rhode Island for the day. Piet, Friedlander and Ramón signed up for something called the Liberty Tour, which actually sounded rather confining. And I went home.

I walked all the way down Fifth; along the Park and past the Plaza and Saint Patrick's. I went past the lions of the library and the Empire State. Then, as the sun seeped through the gauzy sky I crossed the Equator of Fourteenth Street and was back in my native country, the Village.

Washington Square Park was balding and the empty fountain was scarred with graffiti. I stood facing the house on the square where I spent the first twelve years of my life. I wondered if the genteel brownstone was still faculty housing. After all, that's how my parents, both NYU professors, had managed to live in Henry James' world. I think they paid the university some trifling rent to enjoy the most civilized address in Bohemia.

When my mother died of cancer I was in the eighth grade. My father, a classics teacher, seemed to look at me for the first time and realized he'd fathered a child, his only one. I think I actually felt awkward for <u>him</u>. My mother had been almost sole parent while Father gave his classes and tutorials, wrote his essays and spent his summers tinkering around Italy and Greece. Mother had taught child psychology and I had decided not to deconstruct <u>that</u>.

When Father sent me off to Lawrenceville, he shook my hand weakly and handed me a brochure titled *Understanding Male Puberty*. During four years in prep school and four in college he wrote me a letter every two months. And he came to both graduations. The day after the ceremony at Bryn Mawr, in the house I was looking at on Washington Square, he killed himself.

I walked to the corner of Macdougal Street and saw Granados was shuttered.

Throughout the years it had been my canteen and even my pantry if I ran out of wine late at night or I'd forgotten to get bread for a dinner party. My parents had taken me there as a baby and parked the stroller in the sun of West Third Street while they went inside for their five o'clock Negronis. It was during the 1950's and the precursors of the Flower Children were already flaunting their Bloomsbury pedigrees by leaving rows of baby strollers outside ethnic restaurants.

Granados was where I learned about food and wine, slurping down briny oysters with cold flinty white Riojas. It's where the owner, Lorenzo, taught me about *«amor, pesetas y fuerza en la bragueta»*. I wooed a hundred girls in Granados and I can truly say that, while I was in there with them, I meant every word I said.

I went to the West Fourth Street subway station—I wasn't walking sixty blocks back to the hotel. In my hand I had the subway token I bought the day I left for Spain. I rubbed it between thumb and forefinger, feeling the grooved face and the cutout 'Y'. I got to the turnstile and tried to put it in. It wouldn't drop. From the glass booth a huge black woman in oily curls barked into her microphone.

—You tryin' to use old tokens? Retreat from the turnstile now!

That night we met in the sunken bar off the lobby. Cottie bounded in.

—Got the smart spot, guys. Place called Odeon. Pepper steak's the thing.

We talked about how we'd spent our first day. Barbara told us about Joel's parents. Cottie talked about Rhode Island in the snow.

—But tomorrow I'm all business, I'm hitting every publisher in Manhattan. I made ten copies of the manuscript before leaving Madrid.

—And I'm taking my sketches to Donna Karan's people. Spanish *Cosmo* got me the meeting. But that's in the morning. Later I'm doing the JAP tour, Temple Emmanuel, Tiffany's, and Ratner's Deli—Barbara added.

Ramón, Piet and Friedlander looked a little dimmed by their basement-of-the-Federal-Reserve-top-of-the-Empire-State day.

—I think tomorrow we'll just walk. This city sheds its skin every ten blocks—said Friedlander.

—Yes—added Ramón—. With some odd transitions; Little Italy is right next to Chinatown!

—Vut about you, Kevin?

—Oh, I'll do the stations of the cross, Scribner's, Paul Stuart, Balducci's, Ray's Pizza, a movie at the Saint Marks and finally the Met.

Barbara returned from the ladies' room in the lobby.

—You know, this hotel's too good for me. They got rose petals in the toilet bowls.

I looked at the flute of champagne in front of me. Helixes of tiny bubbles sought the surface like strands of golden DNA. I drained the glass.

—Let's go eat.

It was discomfiting not to walk into one of our old haunts for dinner. Now that we didn't have apartments in the city, we assumed that favorite restaurants would be our consulates. In them we could pretend we still lived there; that we'd just been away a bit. We'd be prodigals. And could josh the waiters and the owner and maybe even wave at people we knew. But our safe houses were gone. And we had no time or budget to build up relationships in new places. Because now there were other people doing just that. Taking their turn.

The following morning I woke at six and decided to run in the park. I called the front desk. It was nine degrees outside. I stuffed a towel down my sweatshirt for warmth and skulked through the bright lobby and out into the glacial dark. The sailboat pond was just two blocks away and I ran around it six times, about two miles. But I was having trouble breathing—the air was so cold and sharp. Each time I inhaled it felt like I was breathing in metal filings.

When I got back to the hotel, I met Cottie, who was going in to breakfast.

—Hey, Maestro—he said, pointing at his nose—: watch those hazardous lifestyle choices.

In the elevator I was still breathing hard. And I hunched down because I felt dizzy. Then I saw drops of blood collecting on the floor. I looked in the elevator mirror. My face was totally white, but two streaks of blood poured from my nose. They looked like striations on a gargoyle.

After showering, I looked and felt better. I called Simone Du Lac.

—Kevin! Where are you staying?

I told her.

—Oh, Kevin, that's such an old hotel. I can get you into the Palace. I just put Michael York there.

—This is fine. Want to have a drink later?

—Love to, but can't today. Script meetings. Plus, I'm baby-sitting Robert Blake, whoooooooooo! Why don't—no, I'll call you. It's easier.

Christmas was just two days away and we had talked of spending it in a cabin upstate, roasting a goose and making pies. But that all seemed so contrived now. I walked over to Scribner's on Fifth and joined the shoppers inside the store. There was a giddy, almost manic edge to the crowd that was new to me. I found a copy of Michener's *Iberia* and took my place in line behind a young couple dithering over a gift.

—No, we can't get her the Picasso book. She'll know it's only a hundred dollars. I <u>know</u> her. Let's get her that big book on swimming pools. I think it's <u>two</u> hundred.

The man answered—Pardon the pun, but that seems shallow.

—Okay. Let's get her both!

I stopped at St. Patrick's and heard part of a service. Then I walked down to Paul Stuart for some shirts.

—White cotton, buttoned-down, 15 1/2-32. I need six.

The young salesman took down a folded shirt from the shelf.

—What about that shirt on display?—I asked.

—Well, that's Egyptian cotton, I'm afraid. They'll spoil you for anything else but the problem is they're one-thirty-five—he sighed.

—Is that reverse salesmanship?—I asked.

He pursed his lips and put away the folded shirt.

—Sir, I don't sell. I suggest.

I fortified myself with a thin-crust slice of hot heaven from Ray's Pizza and headed for the revival movie house on St. Marks. It was showing an old Buñuel film shot in Spain. It was easily fifty years old, but the landscapes were unmistakable. So were the people: the angelical laundress, the ferret-like thief.

Then I took a cab to the Met. It wasn't my favorite museum, like Saint Peter's can't be your favorite church. No, the Met is too awesome, too solemn. And I had always 'grazed' there; the Impressionists one day, the Egyptian wing the next. Otherwise, it was indigestible. But that day was different. I felt I could take it all on, even the medieval armor in that Monty-Python gallery.

I went to see the towering Christmas tree they put up every year. But this time I looked at the grilled fence behind it. It had been there all my life, but it was now that I read the plaque. This had been the gated fence that guarded the cathedral of Valladolid before being looted and shipped to America. On that same floor I happened on an entire Andalusian patio, mosaic tiles and potted geraniums included, that I had never seen. Then, upstairs, I found the single most arresting picture in the place: the portrait of Juan Pareja. Not only is it the best Velázquez anywhere, it's as good as any Rembrandt; better, maybe. Because it's 300 years old and it practically breathes in its frame.

I walked back to the hotel, exalted, clutching my *Iberia*.

That evening over drinks we compared our outings.

—These editors!—Fumed Cottie—. They don't even want to look at a manuscript unless it comes from an agent. Now I have to go find an agent.

—At least the people at Donna Karan looked at my sketches—said Barbara, weakly—. Remember the flower-arrangement skirts and those starfish-pattern dresses I thought up in Mallorca? Well, they just wanted to know where my video was.

The others had fared better.

—New York is just diss big buffet and I am a glutton—said Piet, cheerily.

Friedlander was also pleased.

—I discovered an old New York, Trinity Church, McSorley's Ale House ...

Ramón was still taken by the sheer scope of the city.

—It's the creation of someone with Ayn Rand's ideas and Bill Gates' money. My instinctive Spanish reaction, envy, turns to awe.

That night in bed I cracked open *Iberia*, which began with the author's first glimpse of Spain. And I was still reading when sunlight peeked through the curtains around eight. The book had assaulted me with images so astonishing (and yet, knowing what I did of Spain, so probable) that I wondered if I'd just scratched the surface of the country. Michener offered up sketches of places and encounters with people that were simply indelible. And his descriptions—of churches, bullfights, flamenco dancers, a picnic in the country—were so ripe they wafted up from the page.

At breakfast Barbara and Cottie spoke with second-wind brio.

—Hey, if I need an agent to get a publisher, this boy is damn well <u>getting</u> an agent.

—And I'm going to see my uncle Sid—said Barbara—. He knows people in the garment district and those guys don't ask for a <u>video</u>.

—Vut are you doing today, Kevin?

—Well, I walked all around the Village, went to the Met, stopped at Saint Patrick's and I had a slice of Ray's Pizza. So, if I can change my ticket, I may fly back tonight.

Cottie was stunned.

—Kevin, get a grip! Flying back on Christmas Eve? Are you in some Ionesco play? Can there be a more melancholy crew, and pilot, than the ones working that flight? What's wrong with you? Come on, let's get you some eggnog.

When I boarded the 747 that evening, the crew and the pilot were all wearing Santa caps and handing out glasses of champagne. I put my bag in the overhead bin and looked around. There were very few passengers. But I didn't see anyone I would call melancholy. And I had my glorious *Iberia* and I'd be able to stretch across three empty seats. Right before take-off I looked out the window at Manhattan in the distance. It was raining and the view was impressionistic. The skyline looked like birthday candles melting. It occurred to me that Simone had never called me back. That was okay. I couldn't rescue her from the city now, anyway.

—Flight crew, please prepare for arrival.

When the pilot's voice woke me, it was daybreak. I looked out the window at the donkey-colored hills and the brick-red earth of Spain, studded with olive trees. I smiled. It was Christmas morning.

It took only minutes for the taxi to take me home, speeding along the deserted highway and through the quiet streets of Madrid. I sat in the back seat with the window down, getting whipped by the fresh gusts of winter and the smells of the city. As I neared my street the church bells of the old quarter began to peal.

When I got out of the cab I came across my upstairs neighbor, a three-star general named Valcárcel Torregrosa. He was in full-dress uniform and on his way to mass.

—Mr. Byrne, on this very special day for us all, and I know you are a Catholic, I want to wish you the peace of Christ, even in these difficult times of masons and socialists.

When I unlocked my front door, the place seemed eerily quiet. I'd only been gone 96 hours, but not hearing the dogs and not seeing any flowers or any sign of Christmas, it felt abandoned. I tried the kennel: no answer. I'd get Pan and Vino back the next day. I thought about seeing Sonia but she had no phone, so I'd have to walk all the way over there. And it was barely eight o'clock, so I'd just wake her and her brother.

Then it occurred to me that I hadn't spent Christmas Eve in either country; I'd been in the ether. And I wondered if they had any Christmas trees left in the Plaza Mayor. So I walked over there. And I found a tree. And I bought some lights. And I had Christmas.

Chapter Twelve

Sometime in January I got a telex from New York telling me Madrid had been chosen to host that year's board meeting and, in daunting terms, that I would be responsible for the meeting's 'success'. I would have two months to prepare for it. If my company's board members, the WASPiest men in all of Greenwich—wanted to come, then it was impossible to keep Madrid a secret. In fact, Spain itself was being re-discovered. The '92 Olympic games had just been awarded to Barcelona, Sevilla was chosen as the site of the last world's fair of the millennium and Pedro Almodóvar's movies were playing at every mall in Jersey.

Spain was also becoming a magnet for some improbable people. Two of them became acquaintances. Reiko was a graphic designer from Japan who came to me looking for work. Her portfolio was predictably Japanese: immaculate, with a sublime sense of typography and the sheer economy of composition that is the genius of the Japanese. But she spoke zero Spanish at the time and I couldn't throw her in with the groundlings in the studio bullpen nor with the priapic Axis powers upstairs. I gave her a pair of names to call and asked her to keep in touch. There was something about her I liked: the wise face, the long black hair, the short white skirt.

Also by then, the Russians had come. One of them, Vassily, had become Reiko's boyfriend. Now, of all the life strains to seep through the cracks in the Berlin Wall, none was more virulent than the Russian. They charmed you with their brawny good looks, their surprising command of Spanish, and with their wares: the matrioshkas, the scarves, the samovars. All these things, though cheaply made, were novelties in Spain. None of them had any icons or Fabergé eggs, but their mate-y spirit was infectious and from their corners of the park or their makeshift stalls in the flea market, they radiated bonhomie all day long.

At night, however, alcohol transformed them. Then they gushed oaths and dark pronouncements and solemn threats in the bars of Madrid. And that's why I couldn't figure out what the haiku persona of Reiko was doing with the *Gaspadeen* Hyde of Vassily. Reiko had skills. Vassily had penchants. Reiko had an apartment. Vassily had a lifestyle. Like the other Russians, he would arrange his trinkets next to the boat pond in the park and begin to shill. If sales were slow, he and the others would launch into long, mope-y renditions of *Moscow Nights* and *Black Eyes* in their doleful, dirge-y Russian.

One day at a bar in the food market, I asked Vassily what he did with the money from his sales, since he didn't have a dwelling to pay for. He put his face very close to mine and said:

—Ven I sell all the doll and all the Lenin medal and all the scarf, I take room at good hotel. Shoor. I order room service; caviar and vodka. Den I call concierge and order voman. And I spend money until I have just enough to go back to Rosha and start all again.

It was around that time that I began noticing changes in people I'd known for years. One cold morning on Serrano Street I ran into Mar Martínez-Aleya, Randy Blanchard's old girlfriend. She and the aristocrat she left Randy for emerged from a forest-green Range Rover they'd double-parked in front of a florist. Mar saw me and stopped, hesitating for a second before her lips twitched into a smile. I walked over to them.

—Hello, Kevin. How long has it been?

—Almost two years.

—Really? Oh, have you met my husband, Carlos de la Concha y Carbajal?

I shook his hand and noticed how the three C's intertwined on the pocket of his blazer.

—Yes. We met at your show about three years ago. Carlos and I were both admiring your portrait of the queen.

—Heavens, I don't know where we put that old thing. The truth is I haven't painted in a while. I've been busy with other ... works.

She patted her bulging belly with a very ornamented hand.

—I'm expecting in April.

That night I told Sonia about my encounter.

—And she's stopped painting and she was dressed like a forty-year-old. Remember she used to wear those smocks covered with paint smears? Oh, and she was wearing a diamond the size of an ice cube.

—Well, she wouldn't want to get burnt sienna on that, would she?

On the very last day in January, a drippy, foggy afternoon that seemed imported from the Low Countries, I got my first intimation of just how bleak winter could get.

—Hello, Kevin. This is Bill Ellis at the embassy. You might recall we were able to help your friend Randy when he got into a scrape a while back.

I winced and put the receiver to my chest. A few seconds passed before I was able to answer.

—Yes … of course.

—Weeeeell, we've got a little favor to ask, if it's not too much trouble.

—W-what is it?

—You seem to be friendly with, and, hey, it's great to have friends, with Vassily Antipov.

—More with his girlfriend, really. In fact, I don't believe I knew his last name until you told me just now.

—Still, Kevin, didn't you have a drink with him last Tuesday, without the girlfriend?

I didn't say anything.

—See, Kevin, this is real easy. You actually don't need to do anything special. Just keep seeing him and, from time to time, we might ask you what you talked about. That's not so hard, is it?

—That's all?

—Oh, occasionally we might have you ask him something. Something casual. Mundane, even.

My hands turned cold and my mouth was very dry.

—Mr. Ellis …

—Hey, it's Bill. Kevin and Bill. Heh-heh, just a couple of Americans helping each other out in a strange country.

—Well, Bill, I'm not sure I can help you with Vassily. And, to be quite candid, he's the least political guy I know. In fact, he's got a real crush on capitalism, if that helps. Besides, aren't we, I mean the U.S., aren't we friends with the Russians now? Last I heard, we won—right?

—We're friends with everybody, Kevin. Which is why we want to learn more about them.

—And you think I can help.

His voice suddenly hardened.

—He trusts you, son. And, believe me, anybody else just wouldn't smell right to him.

Then his tone suddenly brightened again.

—Don't worry, Kevin. Nobody will feel a thing.

February is just no damn good anywhere.

That year it became known as *El mes de los desastres*. First, dozens died in a disco fire when they swarmed the emergency exits only to find them chain-locked. A Colombian jet crashed three miles short of the airport, killing two hundred. Three days later, two Spanish planes collided on the runway in a thick fog and, rounding out the plagues, the roof on a metro station collapsed, leaving 23 dead under the rubble.

Life seemed especially tenuous, brittle. One saw more car accidents. More people were calling in sick at the agency. One day a large porcelain platter I'd had for years just slid from my hand and shattered. Then, for the first time in my life, I overslept and missed a plane.

On a foggy Sunday morning I went to the flea market for the first time in years. I wasn't looking to buy anything—just wanted to get back in touch with old Madrid, remind myself of the things I liked about the city. The sooty vapor from the coal-burning furnaces blended with the fog and people twenty feet away were just silhouettes. In the Gypsy quarter the tenements were achromatic, like a turn-of-the-century postcard of Warsaw.

At least the Gypsies hadn't changed; proud in their all-black clothes, brass-headed canes and last-legs shoes. But among them I saw new people—lanky, laughing Africans selling necklaces. And sullen, long-maned Andeans in llama-wool ponchos busking on the corner, playing their reedy flutes. These newcomers were different, alien to the Madrid I knew. And I wondered how these young men from Gabon and Peru would get by, especially since it seemed only the men had made the long journey to Spain.

An old Gypsy warmed his hands over a brazier while he guarded his wares—mostly fractions of furniture. One piece was whole: a miniature model of a chair, something cabinetmakers used to carry on their backs as they went from house to house. If someone liked the little chair, a full-scale version would be built back at the shop. The little chair was a bit scuffed, but charming. I offered the gypsy a thousand *pesetas*.

He moved his head to the side and spat. Then he rested both hands on top of his cane and shifted his dentures with his tongue. I moved on.

A half-hour later I walked by the Gypsy again. The little chair was still there. I offered him 2,000 *pesetas*. He tried to get up to run me off. By noon the skies had lowered and it felt ten degrees colder. Some vendors were dismantling their stalls and I decided to head home. Then, on impulse, I thought I'd try again. The Gypsy was huddled close to his brazier and the foot-tall flames rising from it. I was going to offer him 4,000 *pesetas*. But as I came closer, I looked in the brazier and saw the glowing stumps of the little chair.

Leaving the *Rastro*, I passed a dark corner and heard my name. There was an African, big and black as a rotary telephone, wearing shades and an absurd tam-o-shanter. He was in a doorway about ten feet from me. I could have just walked away with the crowd, but there was something commanding in his voice. And he knew my name. He took two steps into the light and smiled, his big yellow teeth like Scrabble chips.

—Ke-veen, your friend brodder need de help.

—Who? Sonia's brother? What's wrong?

—Little brodder got de blues because he need de green. *Comprennez?*

I didn't know whether Pablo really owed him money or this was just a barefaced shakedown.

—What do you want?

—Just 20,000 *pesetas*. But cash, please.

As I looked at him, I remembered: the man in the shadows at the Brazilian dance hall when Pablo asked Sonia for money. Pretty wily of young Pablo to send the collector after me, knowing I'd try to spare Sonia the grief. I looked around. No policemen. Just as well. I dug into my front pocket and took out the bills. I held them out in front of me as far as I could. The African chuckled softly and took the money.

—Well, little brodder now got sponsor.

I walked away quickly and went into the first bar I saw. It was a smoky, rancid cave, but I didn't care. I ordered a scotch. The waiter upended a bottle of domestic whiskey into a tall glass with ice. As the liquor filled it halfway, I raised a palm, a face-saving gesture which in Spain is meant to be ignored. The waiter kept pouring to within an inch of the rim. I took two large gulps and a deep breath. I would say nothing to Sonia.

The following morning I flew up to San Sebastián in a hailstorm that rocked the small Fokker 28. I was calling on my most dubious client, a German who had bribed his way to the concession of an instant-lottery scheme for the Basque country. I felt uneasy about the account and there had been editorials in the local press about *enslaving the populace to a Chimera*. It didn't help that no one had yet won a major prize. I landed in the distinctive *chiri-miri*, that imperceptible drizzle that seems like a fine mist but can add ten pounds to your coat in an hour. San Sebastián was nothing like I remembered from my visit with Mercedes. The alleys of the old quarter were scarred with torn posters and graffiti. The men skulked. And, in the bars, people stopped talking whenever anyone came in. It reminded me of Northern Ireland. After my meeting I walked to the nearest taxi stand. There were no cabs there. The wind was up and all around me in the wet city swirled thousands of gaily-colored lottery tickets torn in two.

On the twenty-third of February, a day that would become iconic in Spanish history, I met Cottie for a drink at the Palace Hotel. There had been problems at work and I'd left the office early, wanting to be with a friend in a comfortable place. The bar at the Palace was thronged with right-wing businessmen and *políticos*—Congress is just across the street—but the place was always *correcto*, right down to the martinis.

—Cheer up, *Consigliere*. You're getting hazard pay, remember? Cottie was referring to that year's bonus. We toasted.

—Hey, look, a napkin poem!

Cottie had found a framed napkin hanging on the wall behind me.

—And it's Lorca's! Come on, translate for me.

I did so while he kept nodding.

—Hmmm. 'I spent my little coins of water drinking at the Palace'. Well, I can do one, too.

He flattened out his cocktail napkin, took a deep breath, and began writing. I turned to the *Tribune* and my martini. After a minute, Cottie drained his glass, stood up and gave me the napkin.

—Here. I'm off to the men's room; cause and effect.

I read the lines.

> *Winter now is like a movie*
> *that starts in an old train station;*
> *black and white and steamy gray,*
> *as Stieglitz saw things. Or was it Steichen?*

I folded it and put it in my pocket.

—Hey, where's my poem?

—Mind if I keep it?

—If you liked the napkin, you'll love the tablecloth—he shrugged

There was a commotion at the door. A waiter ran in from the dining room, his face like an over-exposed photo.

—Mother of God! The Civil Guard has stormed the Congress and taken everyone hostage. It's a coup!

The bartender turned on a small TV behind the bar. The image was in black and white, but unmistakable—the neoclassical facade of the Spanish *Cortes* guarded by the two brass lions. The camera work was shaky and I imagined the operator being jostled and pushed by the Civil Guards streaming into the building.

In the bar men looked up from their evening papers and card games and began approaching the TV. The camera panned to a wind-blown news-caster holding a microphone in one hand and a sheet of paper in the other. He began reeling off what he knew and the paper in his hand was like a tuning fork.

—*... and it seems extremist officers led by General Valcárcel Torregrosa have taken over the chamber, including the president and his cabinet. In fact. the Spanish government is now hostage.*

—Say, Mahatma, did they just mention your upstairs neighbor?

I nodded slowly, still looking at the screen. They were talking about the general I saw every morning leaving with his escort and every Sunday in church, taking communion. Then a brilliantined man with a pencil-thin mustache rose from his banquette. It was Rafael del Molino, a prominent banker and fascist. His eyes were bright. He folded up his copy of the arch-diocese daily and called out:

—*Diego, champán.*

And the old waiter, like a horse with an urge to race after years at pasture, replied:—*Inmediatamente, Don Rafael.*

And, just like that, the eight-year-old Spanish democracy ceased to exist in that room.

I could see into the lobby. Waiters, bellboys and chambermaids rushed past like the cast of an operetta. Del Molino strode to the entrance of the bar and shut the doors.

Cottie discreetly showed me the corner of his passport.

—Think I should ditch this in a potted palm?

—No. I think that might be your get-out-of-jail card.

I started feeling conspicuous and it struck me that Cottie and I were the only ones not wearing neckties.

Del Molino approached and, with excruciating cordiality, addressed me.

—Am I right in thinking you are foreigners?

—Yes, we're Americans.

His smile was sudden and dazzling, like lifting the cover off piano keys.

—Ah, the great Eisenhower! Diego, glasses for our guests—he commanded.

The waiter obeyed at once. It had been years since he'd been ordered around and he'd missed it.

Cottie and I eventually left the hotel through the kitchen. Outside the *Cortes*, the police and the army outnumbered the onlookers. There were tanks up on the sidewalk and two searchlights seared the crowd. It was a cold, blustery night and the air itself felt combustible.

I walked back to my place only to find the entire block cordoned off. A policeman with a machine gun told me I couldn't go near the building. I explained that I lived there and he asked for my *documentación*. He looked at the address on my work permit and up at the number on the building.

He handed back the permit.

—Do you ... know the general?—He asked, softly.

—He's my neighbor ... but I don't know him well.

The policeman looked at me for a few seconds, then snapped his head toward the building. The lobby was thronged with people and there were two women on the sofa in the foyer. I recognized the general's wife. The young woman next to her may have been their daughter. They were both crying.

Much later that night the king appeared on TV in the uniform of commander-in-chief. He told the nation that there was a constitution and there were laws and that was that. Shortly before dawn the insurgents surrendered. I wanted to go out and simply take the pulse of the city. But I didn't want to run into any angry partisans of the failed coup. In Spain, the defeated can be more dangerous than the victors.

I called Ramón.

—Nothing happens. These were madmen, fossilized generals who don't know Franco's dead. After they took over the *Cortes*, there may have been a lot of people sitting on the fence. But once the king went on TV in that uniform, it was all over. The Spanish beast is mortally wounded. This was just a death rattle.

The incident turned out to be a tonic for the young Spanish democracy. People realized just how frail their body politic was and that it still carried a viral gene which could manifest itself at any time.

That week I had three messages from Bill Ellis at the embassy. But I didn't call. Instead I met with Vassily in the park. I told him everything, from my first encounter with Ellis, to his getting Randy Blanchard off the hook and out of the country to his trying to squeeze me into informing on Vassily. I apologized to him.

The big Russian arched his upper body back and looked at me.

—No problem! You are my friend. <u>Good</u> friend. And Vassily know what dis man is and what he want. He spy! Shoor! And he want me to tell about Roshan émigré. Maybe he want Vassily to go to Rosha on mission! Vassily say OK! Why? Because dis man is American. And American always pay. In advance. Hey, maybe he send me to Rosha first-class!

Chapter Thirteen

Around that time I began having problems with New York. Ironically, I was a victim of my success. In my first two years the Madrid office had barely eked out a profit. So to headquarters we were just a pushpin on the map; not profitable enough to be interesting, not losing so much that it required immediate intervention. Of the 167 outposts of the conglomerate we belonged to, only the cash cows and the real dogs got noticed. After the third year, though, Madrid started adding business: first, a beer account, then part of FIAT. Beer and cars are among the biggest advertisers in any country. So the income projections my finance director and I made spiked. And when that happened, New York was watching the seismograph. And I knew what was next.

—Kevin! Todd Bienbach in New York. Howareyaguy? Hey, been going over those financials, great job. Listen, I've been put in charge of emerging markets and I ...

—Excuse me, Todd, I thought emerging markets referred to Eastern Europe ... South Asia.

—Weeeell, any market that's emerging out of the financial doldrums, let's put it that way. And I really want to meet you and get to know the operation in Madrid. How about this Friday? We can meet, spend the weekend together and talk about the future.

—Sounds great—I said.

—So put that in your book, Friday, March 15. Heh-heh, don't read anything into that, Caesar. Oh, can your girl book the hotel and get the tickets from your end? Boss wants the expenses to come out of your kitty. Sorry, *Señor*.

I hung up but I didn't move from my desk. I knew what this was. New York smelled money and they were sending a collector to see how much tribute could be exacted from the Spanish provinces.

—You know, Kevin, we had to lay off 150 people in the New York office. Must feel good to project profit, huh?

He was stroking the leather armrest of the Mercedes 500 I hired to go pick him up.

—Nice car. And a driver, no less. You know, in New York only Roy has a limo with a driver.

—I just hired it for the day. I didn't know if you were coming alone.

—You could have picked me up in your car.

—Well, I don't drive—I shrugged—. New York City kid, never got a license. Besides, don't be impressed because it's a Mercedes. That's what a lot of taxis are here.

—Then we could have taken one. I've only got one bag.

I waited in the car in front of the Ritz Hotel so he could check in and drop off his bag before we went on to the agency. He leaned out from the entrance and called out:

—Hey! They need your credit card to cover the charges.

At the office I showed him the agency showreel and introduced him to some key people, at least those who spoke English. But the only person he wanted to meet was our financial director.

—You don't have to join us, Kevin. I'm sure you have important things to do. And I'm just going to be crunching numbers.

—Well, Todd, I helped prepare those numbers. So I want to be there to make sure they're crunchy enough for you.

He shrugged.

—Suit yourself.

The one restaurant in Madrid all Americans want to go to is Botín. It doesn't matter if you tell them it's a trap, that the food is dismal and the only people they'll see there are other Americans. Botín was mentioned in a Hemingway novel and, seventy years later, the Yanks are still making the pilgrimage, even those who've never read the book. Even those, like Bienbach, who'd never heard of Hemingway.

I brought Sonia along to the dinner, which proved to be a good idea. For a while, anyway. She discovered Bienbach liked movies and they talked about that. When she excused herself from the table Bienbach turned to me and whispered:

—She as hot as she looks? Reminds me of the one in *Quest for Fire*. Ever see that? Huh?

Dinner concluded with Spanish brandies and a group of strolling musicians who, following protocol, left as soon as they were tipped.

—That was great! Yessir, must be nice living here. Y'know what? I'd like to see your place, so I can report back to New York that our people are doing alright here.

At my apartment Bienbach ooh'd and aah'd about the space, the balconies, the high ceilings, the wooden floors and how he'd never seen anything like it.

—Is this your first trip to Europe?—Asked Sonia.

—It sure is. And seeing this place and how you guys live over here, I'm going to consider an overseas posting. But, to be honest, the only place Margie and I would fit in culturally is London.

—Oh? Where do you live now?—Asked Sonia.

—New Jersey.

Bienbach spent the weekend in Madrid watching NBA games in his room at the Ritz. On Monday I went to the hotel to pay his bill and make sure he got to the airport on time. While I waited in the bar downstairs I saw, of all people, Vassily.

—Keveen! Hey, beeg surprise, no? Vassily in Ritz. Beeg stuff, eh?

He was in a black suit and clean-shaven and could have passed for a film star.

—Hey! Touch dis fabric. Brioni, de best.—He looked around the bar and leaned close to me—. I help U.S. now. Shoor. And U.S. help me. Look, American dollar.

He showed me a wad of hundreds.

—U.S. want to know about Roshans here, in embassy. I tell your friend Ellis. Shoor. Why not? Wall come down but nothing change. It's okay. Better for me. Hey, we have drink, Vassily invite.

A week later I was up late, listening to music. I'd been having trouble sleeping and it wasn't unusual to still be up at one or two o'clock, churning work issues and worries. I was concerned that I'd heard nothing from New York after Bienbach's visit and our fiscal year would end March 31st. Maybe they were waiting for my next-year's forecast.

I was listening to Pet Shop Boys when my doorbell rang. I looked at my watch; it was one-thirty. I thought it might be Sonia.

—I'm coming.

I opened the door and there, with a face streaked by make-up and tears, was Reiko. She stood, trembling and with clenched fists.

—They kirr Vassiry!

If that winter had a soundtrack for me it would include songs like *Time After Time, Here Comes The Rain Again,* and the Cars' haunting *Drive,* all of them plaintive and cautionary. If things seemed dismal in January and February, they were positively dire by March. I began having premonitions, not just about work, but about Spain in general. And it wasn't that I detected any particular gloom or threat. It was the opposite: there was a manic euphoria I'd never seen in Spain. And it seemed fueled by the country's new visibility: the coming Olympics, the World's Fair, the bullet train, the international cachet of Real Madrid's team, Almodóvar's movies and Julio Iglesias' voice. Spain was 'in' and Spaniards were on a spree.

The week before I sent our final forecast to New York, I met with my financial director, José Maestre. Pepe was typical of all the accountants I was to meet in Spain: dour, cautious, pessimistic. But at that meeting he was practically ebullient.

—Look, Kevin, if just these three accounts spend as much next year as they did this year, we could make a profit of 150 million *pesetas.* That's a million dollars!

I looked at the list.

—Pepe, all three of those were government campaigns, this one for Valencia oranges, that one for *manchego* cheese, and the third one to boost consumption of Spanish fish.

—So?

—Tell me, Pepe, what other kind of fish are Spaniards going to eat? What other kind of oranges or cheese, for that matter? Listen, Pepe, it's not just that those campaigns are completely superfluous, it's that the government shouldn't be wasting all that money on vainglorious messages for domestic consumption. They should be trying to sell all those products, sure, but overseas! Look, it's not healthy for any agency to have so much riding on advertising revenue that is politically motivated. If this government loses the next elections, the new party will undo everything this one did. That revenue could evaporate. Do me a favor, don't include any projected income from those three campaigns in the forecast we send to New York next week.

—But why?

—Because ... because I say so.

I wanted to meet with Ramón Cuevas and get his thoughts. So I invited him to lunch at Galería, a place that was itself iconic of the rabid consumption then in Spain. It was a two-tiered mall-in-the-round that included Bulgari, Prada and Godiva. There was even a Ferrari dealership on the ground floor.

—How does all this look to you, Ramón?

He looked around.

—Like Pompeii before Vesuvius. But, then again, I've not been to Las Vegas.

—But is this sustainable? Can Spaniards actually shop here?

—Kevin, one of my neighbors in Chinchón, he grows cabbages, just bought a BMW. The only thing he's ever driven in his life is a tractor.

—I know, my housekeeper got an American Express card! What do people say at the paper?

—Well, all the editors except one seem to believe in the boom. They're buying up all the bond issues that come to market.

—But, Ramón, those are all ultimately government bonds. Even if they're issued by the airline or the railroad or the oil company, who the hell owns Iberia, Renfe and Repsol? The government! They're strapped, so they're raising money! If the socialists get kicked out, is the right-wing party going to pay off on those bonds?

—Well, since I work for the socialist paper, it's not a question I can ask.

—You said there was one editor who wasn't buying the new prosperity.

—Yes. Ironically, it's the financial editor. But management has reassigned him. The worrisome part is not that people with some money are spending it; it's that people with no money are spending it, too. A secretary at the paper is having her wedding abroad.

—So?

—In Kenya? A girl who's never even been to Barcelona is having a wedding safari? By the way, are your clients spending?

I told him about the government campaigns and that I felt they were unlikely to repeat.

—Ah, Kevin, that is how the government keeps the peace in the provinces. It gives the *gallegos* millions to advertise their shellfish, the *valencianos* more millions to sing the praises of their oranges and the *andaluces* even more millions to celebrate the virtues of their olive oil and ham.

—Wonderful products all of them! But why preach to the choir? Advertise in France, in England. Or advertise in the U.S.! Wine consumption in America has gone up 40% in five years. Why are the French getting all that business when Spain has just as good a product at half the price?

Ramón smiled and lit a Ducados.

—But if they advertised abroad, the people those messages are meant to flatter and whose loyalty they're designed to suborn, wouldn't see them.

—Ramón, I know enough about economics to tell you no free-market economy should have the government as its biggest advertiser. It should be the private sector. It's a very unhealthy situation.

—You're right, Kevin. And the financial editor told me he fears a complete crack sometime this year.

—What does he think will happen?

—Well, the socialists have been spending their way to popularity, just to secure the votes in the south, that's their base. They've spent billions on the world's fair that's coming to Sevilla. And billions more on the bullet train to the coast. Who needs a bullet train to go to the beach? They should have built it between Madrid and Barcelona, the two business capitals. And the government is spending a huge amount on the Olympics this summer. All these Pharaonic projects could break the bank. In which case, not only will government advertising evaporate, but social services will, too.

—Why doesn't the opposition party blow the whistle on these guys?

—They try. But look.

He held up his paper's front page. There was a photo of a leading opposition figure and the caption read:

—Fraga, looking tired and emotional.

—Do you know that euphemism? It means the guy was drunk.

I shook my head.

—So what's going to happen? When I came to Spain this was a fiscally conservative country. Hell, you needed three permits to buy dollars at a bank. And now, look at the people in those stores.

Ramón sighed.

—Spain's problem is that we've jumped from the washbowl to the shower gel without having used Lagarto soap.

—Oh, well. Let's order. I've got to get back to the office.

Ramón perused the menu and his brow began to furrow.

—If you think the new profligacy of the Spaniards is worrisome, there are even more alarming trends. Look at this.

He held the menu open before me and exclaimed with distaste:

—*Quiche!*

In the morning I flew to Bilbao, the brooding industrial city of the north, to meet with some potential clients. A group of bankers and industrialists, sober stewards of the city, were actually going to build a branch of New York's Guggenheim Museum in Bilbao. And they were going to do it with private funds. I spent most of the day plotting out what I thought should be their marketing strategy, in Spain and abroad. I suspected they wanted to launch a big splashy visitor magnet both to restore the tourism that had evaporated as a result of separatist violence and to simply say: Bilbao is important; Bilbao *matters*.

By five o'clock, our business concluded, they shook my hand and wished me a safe trip. Anywhere else in Spain, at that hour, the clients and I would still be at some restaurant prolonging lunch with a sampling of liqueurs and, if the mood struck, coming at last to the matters we'd been neglecting all day.

I took a cab to my hotel. Bilbao, devoted to the two faiths of finance and steel, sits on the banks of the gray and sluggish Nervión River. It is not a walker's city. But I'd found a traditional Basque guesthouse in the well-tended suburb of Neguri. I had an early supper in the dining room, where only two other tables were occupied; one by a group of traveling salesmen, the other by a British woman dining alone. As in most Basque restaurants, the servers were all women, young girls in aprons and coifs. And the lettering on the menu, as well as all the signage in the hotel, was in that quaint typography that suggests letters hand-carved with an axe. In addition to the other idiosyncrasies of the Basque country, they also had their own typeface.

I asked the waitress to bring me coffee and a cognac to the lounge. I sat on a sofa by the crackling fireplace, near a table with a sorry array of very old magazines about farming and animal husbandry. A few minutes later the British woman entered the lounge. She looked down at the magazines.

—I'm afraid they don't have *Tatler*—I said.

—That's quite all right. I have a book I've been avoiding. May I sit down?

—Please. What brings you to Bilbao?

—A medical convention. I'm a doctor, Sarah Poole.

I extended my hand.

—Kevin Byrne. Will you have coffee or a liqueur?

—No, thanks. I have an early flight back to London. I just came in here for the fireplace.

She looked around the alpine-y lounge.—This isn't what one pictures when one thinks of Spain, is it?

—No. I think the Basque Country looks more like parts of Britain than like any other part of Spain—I said.

—Perhaps that's why the separatists don't become … assimilated.

—Well put, Doctor. They are not 'assimilated' at all.

Just then, the receptionist walked into the lounge and closed the doors behind him. He was a young pale man with a blinking tic. He spoke in halting English.

—Pardon me, Madame. I see you assist to the medical congress. Are you a doctor?

—Yes, I am.

—Er …—he looked at me entreatingly—. *¿Me podría traducir al inglés?*

—*Claro*. He asked me to translate.

—*Hay un hombre en el hotel que necesita un médico.*

—He says that a man in the hotel needs a doctor.

—Well—she said—. I can take a look. Let's go to his room.

The receptionist understood that much.

—*Dígale que no está en una habitación … está en el sótano.*

I paused a few seconds.

—It appears the man is not a guest of the hotel. He's in the basement.

—The basement? Why? What's wrong with him? Can't he be moved?

—*Dígale que … hay mucha sangre.*

—He says there's quite a bit of blood.

She sighed.

—Well, I'll go have a look. Could you come along to translate?

—Of course.

We walked down narrow stairs to a low, dank room. The only light came from an oil lamp on the earthen floor. A heavyset man with a beard and a woman with long hair stood by the wall, with their hands in their pockets. They said nothing. Another man, pale and perspiring, lay under a blanket on a bunk bed. The receptionist nodded quickly at the doctor and me and hurried up the stairs. I heard the large wooden door to the basement lock above us.

Calmly, Doctor Poole approached the bunk bed. She placed one hand on the man's forehead while she took his pulse with the other. Then she pulled back the blanket. He wore a rough denim shirt stained with a red that was almost black. The bearded man and the woman moved closer to her, still saying nothing. Doctor Poole unbuttoned the shirt gingerly and opened it. Now we could all see it; the red-stained abdomen and the bright brimming hole.

—Puncture wound—said the doctor. She turned to me—. Ask them if this was a hunting accident.

I looked at the couple, who looked both fearsome and frightened.

—No, Doctor, I'm sure this wasn't a hunting accident.

That morning there had been a skirmish just across the French border and anti-terrorist forces were looking for three people.

Doctor Poole sat on the edge of the bunk and looked at the man.

—Tell him I'm going to feel around the wound and that he'll have some discomfort.

I translated and the man nodded quickly.

The doctor's fingertips moved around the puncture. The man yelped and exclaimed an oath between clenched teeth. Doctor Poole looked at me.

—There's a subcutaneous projectile. He'll have to go to the hospital.

—¡NO!—The bearded man had at least understood that last word. He turned to me with a menacing look—. *Aquí no va nadie a ningún hospital. ¿Me entiendes, tío?*

I looked at the doctor.

—Um ... the hospital is out.

Doctor Poole said:

—Then there's nothing I can do. I have no instruments and, besides, these aren't the conditions under which to clean and dress that wound. And that wound, if untreated, will turn septic.

—*Pregúntale qué necesita*—blurted the bearded man.

—He wants to know what you would need.

The doctor turned to the ceiling with exasperation and then faced me.

—Everything! Tweezers, a surgical needle and sutures, sterilized dressing and some type of anesthetic ... lidocaine or fentanyl; and, ideally, a tetanus vaccine.

—*Que haga una lista. Despertaremos al farmacéutico del pueblo.*

—He wants you to list the items. He'll wake the local pharmacist.

She looked at me with cold gray eyes.

—Mister Byrne, can you tell me what this is all about?

—Well, Doctor, I think this is one of those failures to assimilate that we spoke about upstairs. And, quite candidly, I suggest you do the best you can. And I admit I have selfish reasons for saying that.

Two hours later, Doctor Poole had extracted a bullet from the man's body and had cleaned and closed the wound. She bandaged the man, who looked much better by then, and announced:

—There. That is all I can do here. Please tell them that the wound needs a dressing change daily. But I expect no complications.

The bearded man approached me slowly.

—*Oye, tú, le dices que se lo agradece el pueblo vasco.*

—He says the Basque people offer you their gratitude.

The doctor was scrubbing her hands with rubbing alcohol, but stopped, and looked witheringly at the bearded man.

—Tell him I didn't do it for 'the Basque people'. I took an oath.

The man detected her contempt, but shrugged and turned to me.

—*Oye, tío, aquí no ha pasado nada, ¿vale?*—He poked a hard finger in my chest.

By then it was three in the morning and I decided to stay up. I watched the fireplace die out while I soothed my nerves with Jan Morris' lyrical, reassuring book, *Spain*.

At daybreak, I went up to my room to shower and pack. Downstairs, the receptionist quietly told me than a hotel employee would take me and Doctor Poole to the airport. When I asked for the bill, he said both mine and the doctor's had been 'taken care of'.

In the car to the airport, Doctor Poole suddenly turned to me and said:

—You know, whatever their grievance is, they have no right to implicate innocent strangers.

—Well, they might tell you that theirs is a universal cause; that it's everyone's struggle.

—Rubbish! They're a bunch of thugs—she looked out the window at the drippy landscape and murmured—: and I don't mind telling you … I was rather scared during the whole thing.

—You could have fooled me, Doctor. But I guess that's what Brits are famous for: grace under pressure.

She shot me an incredulous glance and exclaimed:

—Bollocks!

Chapter Fourteen

On the last night in March I sat in my apartment, sheltered from a late-winter hailstorm. The naked branches of a maple drummed at my living room window and the wind whistled through the doors to the balconies. Sonia must have guessed at my mood because she called to say she was coming over. I opened a bottle of Viña Ardanza, my favorite wine, but I hardly drank. I walked over to the bookshelves and thought about revisiting an old stand-by, Maugham or Irwin Shaw; a good storyteller to beguile me from my gloom.

I went to answer the doorbell. Sonia came in, wearing a yellow hooded rain slicker. Her caramel face was beaded with water and curls framed her forehead and cheeks. She looked up at me with large, lambent eyes.

—¡Ay, mi niño!

Then, without removing her rain gear, she strode to the living room, where the sound system issued one of Depeche Mode's narcoleptic odes. She turned it off.

—That's the trouble, you sit up here by yourself listening to that stuff. Of course it gets you down. Should I be searching for an empty bottle of pills?

I half-smiled.

—Nope. <u>You're</u> my bottle of pills.

She came toward me and wrapped me in a hug.

—And my bottle of wine ... my tin of caviar ...

Her cheeks were cold but her hair smelled warm, like cinnamon.

—You're my gold card.

—Well, you just remember that and forget about your job. You know, you should get out of Madrid, get out in the country. See some cows!

—Not now. This is a busy time. I turned in financials today, board's meeting in Madrid next month and I haven't prepared a program.

—Well, you need to look past all that. Is there something else you're looking forward to?

—Hmmm ... actually, there is.

—Is it something wonderful?

—To me it is.

—Well, then put it in your thoughts right now, concentrate on it.

I closed my eyes, still hugging her.

—I'm concentrating.

—Is it giving you pleasure just thinking of it?

—Very much.

—Is it ... exciting?

—Thrilling.

—Tell me what it is.

I opened my eyes.

—Tomorrow is the start of the baseball season.

She slapped my chest and pulled away. Then she laughed and came to me again. And we hugged again, rocking gently right and left. And she kissed me with her warm, cushy mouth and it felt as electric as the first time; as every time. And I hadn't noticed the phone was ringing.

I picked up the wall phone in the kitchen.

—*¿Sí?*

There was some very loud music and voices at the other end. I thought it might be Cottie or Barbara calling after a few drinks. It was past one o'clock.

—Anybody there?

—Ke-veen ... Ke-veen.

I went cold. That deep, rumbling voice: the African from the *Rastro*.

—What do you ... how'd you get this number?

—Little brodder. He need your help again ...

—Where are you? Is he with you? I must speak to him!

Sonia had heard me growing excited on the phone and she came silently to my side. I cupped my hand over the receiver.

—Don't worry. Wait for me in the living room. Get us both a glass of wine.

She slipped away.

—You can talk when you come. You know Baby Q?

—The disco, on the Coruña road. Yes, I know it!

—Then come, but be sure you bring 50,000 friends with you.

The line went dead.

I went back to the living room.

—Put that jacket back on.

—What? Are we going out? In this weather?

—Yes. Come on.

—Where are we going?

I hurriedly put on my coat and grabbed a cap from the closet. At that hour and with the rainstorm I knew we'd never find a cab.

—Can you drive?—I asked.

—Yes, I can drive. But I don't have a car and neither do you.

—There's a 24-hour AVIS at the train station. Let's go.

—But tell me why!? Where are we going?

—I'll tell you on the way.

At the station Sonia got a VW Golf and a road map while I assaulted an ATM. The roads were fairly empty but the rain was coming down hard.

—Take the next exit, the Coruña road. And don't go over 80; there are no streetlights and the road surface is like motor oil.

—Kevin, you've got to tell me where we're going!

I told her. Everything; about the encounter at the flea market and the 20,000 pesetas. And about the phone call now. What I didn't tell her was about my dread. Not having actually spoken with her brother, I couldn't be sure he was even there. Or even alive.

Sonia said nothing. She drove on grimly, tightening her grip on the wheel. But her eyes were on fire.

—Sonia, let's just get him out of there tonight. Tomorrow we'll think about next steps, okay? Maybe we go to the police or we take him to a clinic or … I don't know. But I promise I'll help you through this.

A sudden burst of lightning flared before us and I could see the tears that streaked her face. The rain had gotten worse.

—Use your brights. Can you find them?

She turned them on and, immediately, another vehicle about 100 yards ahead turned its own brights on.

—God, why did they do that? Quick, turn yours back down. Can you see the car coming?

—Y-yes, it's a big truck. But why is he going so fast?

—Quick! Flash your lights at him!

—Why is he driving so close to the line!?

—Move to the right as far as you can! Now!

There was a long urgent horn that rent the night and the brights from the truck came right upon us and the crash was so loud I thought the night itself was broken and the last thing I remember thinking about was the saltiness of one's own blood.

SPRING
(One Month Later)

Chapter Fifteen

Sacred Heart Hospital, a former convent, has a pleasant interior courtyard, one of the quietest places in Madrid. I could hear the conversation between a woman in a wheelchair and her dutiful daughter, who pushed gently along the rose bushes. Two men in bathrobes, one of them with an oxygen tank, talked in adjoining chairs. And, sitting on the rim of the fountain, a priest was hearing the confession of a gaunt young man. I sat on a bench under the eager but ineffective sun of April. While I waited for my visitor I re-read a letter left for me three weeks earlier.

Esteemed Mr. Byrne: I had hoped you would regain consciousness before I returned to the Basque Country. I wanted to thank you for what you were trying to do—I have spoken to Pablo. He is in Carabanchel Prison along with the African who was extorting you. I wish you and I could have made the arrangements for my daughter together. She had told me of your mutual affection and I derived some paternal serenity from it. Now I will take Sonia's ashes to my home in Bilbao. This summer I will cast them where her mother lies, in Cienfuegos, Cuba. Sonia was so very much like her mother. I still can't believe I've lost them both. But they say being Basque means knowing the world will one day break your heart. I wish you a full recovery and ask you to keep Sonia in your prayers, which I know you will. Attentively, Andoni Mondragón.

José Maestre, pale and sheepish, had arrived.

—Hello, Kevin. How are you feeling today?

—I'm better, Pepe. Thank you.

He sat down across from me and was silent for a few seconds.

—Pepe, I think I know why you're here. Please, look at me.

He raised his doleful eyes.

—Pepe, do you have an envelope for me?—I asked, as though cajoling a conscience-stricken nephew.

He nodded and handed it to me.

Dear Kevin: It is with regret that I inform you of my decision to relieve you of your duties at our Madrid office, effective immediately. The timing of this letter is most unfortunate, as I'm told you're still recovering from your injuries. In your final forecast I've learned you ordered the financial director, despite his entreaties, to omit projected earnings from three substantial accounts—ones which contributed handsomely to the agency's performance last year. This suggests two disturbing possibilities. Either you lack confidence in retaining them or, as we've been told, you lack confidence in the future of Spain itself. And if a leader is less certain than the people he leads, then he shouldn't be in that position. In fact, Todd Bienbach recommended that the Madrid office be led by a local. I am sending him to Madrid this week to become acting director and to conduct an executive search. I hope you look at this as an opportunity to reassess your career and to consider if Spain is indeed the best professional environment for you. I want to thank you for your past service and wish you a complete recovery.

It was signed by Roy Wheatley, CEO of the international network.

I fixed my stare on Pepe, which he must have taken as an indictment.

—Kevin, they interrogated me! I was afraid … I have four children!

—Pepe, relax—I patted his knee.

—I … I have another envelope—he said.

It was the severance check.

—It is all there, the full compensation. I told them not to contest it, for they would surely lose in the labor tribunals.

The amount was very substantial. For once, I endorsed Spain's labor laws.

—I could have come by for it, Pepe.

—Well, they wanted it this way. And they told me to pack your office things and send them to your apartment.—He bowed his head—. I'm sorry, Kevin.

—Don't be. I'll be leaving the hospital soon. Then I'll be on vacation—I held the check up—. Paid vacation.

He rose and extended his hand. I shook it.

—Kevin, I wish to give you something. It is not habitual in Spain for men to give such things, but please accept it.—He put a small velvet pouch in my hand and closed my fingers over it.

I smiled.

—Pepe, why the gift?

He turned to leave and looked back at me. His eyes were red-rimmed.

—Because I know you love my country—He left, treading softly on the gravel. I emptied the pouch. It was a Saint Christopher medal.

The health code for all state clinics in Spain stipulates that no patient can be discharged from the trauma unit without the approval of a doctor in the counseling services; in other words, a psychiatrist. I reported to the office of *Doctora* Rosa Palomar. It was small and austere and may have been one of the bedchambers when the building was a nunnery. It had an ascetic feeling still: bare cement floors, a pinewood desk and a chair, one row of books and just one picture—a black-and-white photo of a house. The doctor looked to be in her forties, with large patient black eyes and hair trimmed almost to the scalp like a salt-and-pepper helmet on her handsome face. She wore only one earring, a long silver pendant that could have been a Brancusi.

She sat down behind her desk with no papers or charts. She folded her hands together and gazed at me with wise, knowing eyes.

—Tell me, how are you feeling today?

—Physically?

—And mentally. Describe your state of mind.

—Well ... grateful, I guess. I'm alive. I've almost recovered, except my right arm still hurts, so I tend not to use it.

—I'll recommend a physical therapist for that. But I'd like to know what you plan to do once discharged. The hospital has been informed you're no longer working.

—Oh. Does that mean my treatment isn't covered?

—Don't worry. You're protected by social security. I was wondering to what extent losing your job affects your outlook. How do you feel about the future?

She framed her face with a thumb and forefinger.

—I'm not ... daunted by it, or anything.

—Tell me, you were an only child and both your parents are dead. You have listed no living relatives in your dossier. And in a society as dispersed as America's, that means you're really quite alone, aren't you?

For an instant, I didn't know if that was a trick question. What if I did say I felt alone? Would they not discharge me? What if I put on an air of breezy confidence and replied: alone but never lonely? Would she think I was in denial?

—I'll sign the discharge papers. But you need to see our physical therapist, two floors up. Take this form.

—Thank you. May I ask you a question?

—I ask all the questions in this room—she said, sternly. Then she laughed, a warm, throaty laugh—. I was joking. Ask.

—Where is that house in the photo? It looks so peaceful.

—It's a cottage I have on the island of Menorca, in a town called Horizonte.

—Never been there, I've been to Mallorca, though.

She waved a dismissive hand in the air, and half-a-dozen bangle bracelets chimed prettily.

—Nothing to see. Menorca is all wilderness and wind. And not one single German.

She extended her hand.

—Good luck, Kevin Byrne. If you ever think talking to someone like me might help, don't put it in doubt.

I found the physical therapy department and knocked. A very young-sounding voice called out:

—Forward.

—I entered a room that was more like a small gym. A compact but strong-looking blonde sat at a table wearing a red leotard beneath her white tunic. Her hair sprayed out from a delicate face in long, tight curls, so it looked like a golden fern. Her eyes were arctic blue.

—Counseling services sent me. I was in a bad car accident and I'm afraid my right arm suffered. It hurts when I move it, so I tend not to use it.

She sprang from behind the table.

—Large mistake. If you don't use it, it will atrophy. Raise it for me, please. Point to the ceiling, stretch it as far as you can.

—Ow. That hurts.

—Can you do a windmill motion with your arm?

—Only while screaming.

—Hmmm. The best treatment is aquatic therapy. I'm at the Omega pool on Fridays. Call for an appointment. Don't preoccupy yourself. Your arm will fully recover.

—That eases my mind.

—I don't see how. I'm a *physical* therapist.

She gave me her card.

—Hmmm, Claudia Muntaner. Are you *catalana*?

—As the sky is blue.

Back in my apartment, I looked at the boxes with the contents of my former office. For a minute I considered just having the doorman throw them all in the trash. After all, there was no point in finding room for things in a place I might have to vacate. But I knew that, among the hundreds of blithering memos and laughably irrelevant documents, there might be a book or a photo I'd like to rescue.

There was a knock on the door.

—Barbara. Come on in, mind the boxes.

—Wow! Are you leaving, too?

—No, no. It's the stuff from my office.

—I heard. I'm sorry, Kev. You know, I did go by the hospital to tell you I was leaving; but you were out of it.

—Well, I'm here now. Want a drink?

—No, thanks. I've just got a few minutes. But I didn't want to leave town without seeing you.

—Where will you go?

—Well, I hear Prague's really happening. Some people say Berlin's the place now—she looked at me with earnest blue eyes—. Kev, I'm not telling you what to do, but maybe Madrid's moment has come and gone. Like London in the '60s after Carnaby Street, or New York in the '70s after Studio 54. Maybe the '80s were Madrid's time ... and, well, time's up—her mouth quivered into a smile—. In any case, a girl's gotta stay with it—and her eyes crinkled at the corners.

That morning I went to the kennel to retrieve Pan and Vino. Cottie had taken them there after the accident. Then I went to the bank to deposit my severance check. I didn't want to carry it around any longer. At the BBV branch near Alcalá I approached my longtime teller, Ángel, and told him what happened. He was inexplicably moved.

—Kevin, I will take a break now. Let me invite you to a coffee.

At the bustling café, Ángel suggested that I convert the check from *pesetas* to dollars or pounds.

—You're a foreigner. By law, you can repatriate your money in another currency whenever you like—he looked up and down the busy counter and, lowering his voice, said—: I think it would be prudent.

So, after our coffees—and two mid-morning brandies—we went back to the bank and I wired 20 million *pesetas* in dollars to my U.S. account. It was received within minutes. I kept seven million *pesetas* in Spain, which I thought should see me through the year, when my work and residence permits would expire, anyway.

That night on TV, they announced the resignation of the governor of the Bank of Spain. I called Ramón.

—What's going on?

—The rumor at the paper is that he wanted to declare a devaluation but the president wouldn't let him.

—What's the problem with the *peseta*?

—The socialists have been propping it up, buying *pesetas* with their foreign reserves. Now the reserves are gone. So now it's going to float out there on its own.

The next day, Friday, was a holiday, so Spain had a three-day weekend.

But in the rest of Europe, the major exchanges reported heavy trading in *pesetas*. On Wall Street the *peseta* lost 18% of its value in one day. I called my bank in New York. The wire transfer had been credited to my account the day before, at the old exchange rate. I made a mental note to buy Ángel a new car.

On Saturday I met Piet van Doornen and Robert Friedlander at Galería for drinks. Piet was returning to Amsterdam and Friedlander was going back to London. There were lots of empty tables and I found we could talk without raising our voices, which was a first in Galería.

—Yah, I got calls from Amsterdam now. Ver vur dey tree years ago? Ah, it dussn't matter—said Piet.

Friedlander sipped his sherry and commented wryly:

—And I've been summoned back by the photo agency that wouldn't take my calls when I lived there.

On Sunday I went to the Prado. I needed to look at Goya again; to see why Sonia had thought him the best painter in the place. And I confronted the two Goyas—first, the harrowing paintings downstairs. I drank in their darkness: *Saturn Devouring His Son*, and that glimpse into the genius of Spanish savagery, *Duel With Cudgels*. But upstairs, the 'other' Goya washed over me: one big, bright canvas after another, visions of Arcadian bliss in blues and pinks. Were the people in those paintings—celebrating the grape harvest, playing with their barnyard animals—Spaniards, also? And what about Goya himself? Who was he when he painted these bucolic paragons and who was he when he made *Los Desastres De La Guerra*? Maybe that's why Sonia thought him a great master; because he depicted the raging duality of his people. It reminded me of another Spanish artist, the Romantic poet Becquer, who could be euphoric on one page and hopeless on the next. How often I'd seen examples of those pendular swings, even among the Spaniards of today; a person unshakably self-centered could also perform acts of staggering generosity. It led me to an oft-reached conclusion: Spaniards are simply incalculable.

I hadn't seen Cottie since leaving the hospital, so we arranged to meet that afternoon at Bar Hispano. I was taking a *Herald Tribune* from the newspaper rack when the doors opened and in strode a tall female lieutenant in uniform, with a black beret, Army boots and a NATO patch on her shoulder. Cottie came in behind her.

—Okay, Officer—I asked—, what's he done now?

The woman, blue-eyed and fine-featured, squinted at me and hissed:

—Insubordination.

I extended my hand.

—Kevin Byrne.

She shook it.

—Kelly Cochran.

—Hey, *Commendatore*, how are ya?—Cottie and I bumped up against each other in a near-hug.

We ordered drinks and *tapas*.

—Man, your face looks great. At the ICU the morning after the crash it looked like a Francis Bacon portrait.

—How's your pitching arm?—Asked the lieutenant, seeing my right hand was bandaged.

—Iffy. I don't think I'll be ready for the crucial Red Sox series.

She drained her beer and stood up.

—Gotta go. I've heard a lot about you, Kevin. I hope to see you again.

Cottie stood up and they kissed quickly. Then she bounded up the steps and into the street.

—Is that on the menu?—I asked, popping an olive.

—Well—replied Cottie—, I'd tried all the pick-up lines in the world, but there's nothing like yelling:

—SIR! REQUEST TO BE EMBEDDED WITH SIR, SIR!

I smiled. We sipped our drinks in the feeble light that seeped through the windows. We sat silently, as true friends can without becoming uncomfortable. Cottie spoke first.

—Hey, *Maréchal*, I'm really sorry about Sonia.

—They gave me your letter. It helped. Really.

—And together, I thought you'd both hit the lottery.

—Yeah. I ... I felt for once I was truly giving someone something, not just ... getting.

—Do you know what you'll do now?

—Severance will carry me for a while. Work and residence permits expire at the end of the year, anyway, unless some other company hires me.

—Don't you fret, Herr Oberst—said Cottie, raising his glass—you're going to ace this.

—Thanks for the faith. Oh, and thanks for taking the dogs to the kennel and looking after the apartment.

—*Au contraire, mon frère.* For a month I told every woman I knew that it was my place.

Chapter Sixteen

The first radiant morning of spring arrived that Monday. I opened the doors to the balconies and a moist breeze wafted over from the park. My potted geraniums were sweating dew in the sunlight and a butterfly perched briefly on my arm.

I had an appointment with an executive recruiter at ten and I left my place early so I could walk there. I stopped at my newsstand on Alcalá and saw a long line of people outside the Santander bank on the corner.

—Are they giving away paella pans again?—I asked the vendor.

He frowned and gave me my change.

—They're all making withdrawals. There's talk of a devaluation, so they figure it's better to spend what they have now.

I went into a bar for a coffee. The TV was on and the minister of finance was announcing that the stock exchange would remain closed for the day—to assimilate financial corrections caused by foreign markets. I called Ramón.

—Do you want a translation? The *peseta*'s going to hell but it's the rest of the world's fault. I have a friend at the ministry and she says things are so bad people are stabbing each other in the <u>front</u>. So they bring out the minister because the president doesn't have the gills to give the face.

Lander and Company is an international executive recruiter with an office in Madrid. My appointment was with Elena Sotomayor, the dauphine of the fabled dynasty of Spanish lawyers. She already had my dossier, including the letter of dismissal from New York.

—Very well, Mr. Byrne—she said while she swiveled in her chair, staring me down—. You were a political casualty, correct? Your company wanted to bet on black and they fired you for betting on red. Yes or no?

—Well … it's not that I don't believe in Spain, but …

—LIE!—She slammed her palm on the table and jumped out of her seat. Then she began circling my chair—. You don't believe in our economy. Period!

—Well, I think ...

—I AGREE! The socialists are a disaster and this economy is a mirage. God knows what's really going on with the *peseta*. But let's get back to you. You, the you in this folder, are the product I have to sell. And if that product is a *Yanqui* who, on top of that, is also a financial pessimist ... well, not a seductive résumé so far, eh?

She sat on the edge of her desk and looked down at me. It occurred to me that she'd be formidable in a courtroom.

—Mr. Byrne, what is your chief objective?

—I want to stay in Spain.

She howled.

—It has screwed us! Of course you do, piece of an idiot! But to do that you first must get someone to give you a job!

She jumped off the edge of the desk and began circling my chair again and I realized that behind the bluster and the volcanic energy was actually an exceptionally fine-looking woman with swimming-pool blue eyes and flawless white skin.

—Kevin, Madrid is not a receptive market for you right now. But I will explore some possibilities. It helps that your Spanish is excellent—she stood behind my chair and put a hand on my shoulder—. *Vas a superar esto*, Darling.

I turned to face her.

—So there's hope for me?

—Well, this is Lander, not Lourdes.

I walked home, oddly buoyed by the encounter. On Paseo de Recoletos waiters were setting tables outside for the first time all year. And I saw my first mime of the season, a gamine completely painted in silver, pretending to be a fairy. Further on, a raggedy string quartet was tuning up behind a battered violin case they hoped to fill with coins. I waited until they began with, fittingly, Vivaldi (blessedly un-amplified), and I dropped a 100-*peseta* coin in the violin case. As I walked home I caught myself whistling. And I am not, by nature, a whistler.

That Friday I went to my first aquatic therapy session. Claudia Muntaner, in a severe black bathing suit, directed me from the edge of the pool. She had me dog-paddle for a few laps, then switched me to the breaststroke. I felt fine until she called for a backstroke. Pain bolted through my arm. I stopped altogether and just stood in the water a few seconds. She put her clipboard down, sprang into the pool and streaked thirty feet underwater, like a dolphin, to emerge right next to me.

—Here, first extend your arm straight up. Higher.

—That hurts.

—Of course it hurts.

—That's your best poolside manner?

—Your body has to learn these movements again. Your body has forgotten.

—Let it have amnesia.

—No. Use your shoulder blade to ease your arm back. I'll show you.—She put a very strong hand under my right shoulder blade and, with her other hand, maneuvered my arm back gradually. It still hurt, but I was very distracted by her scent.

After 20 minutes I got out and began drying off while she looked at me.

—Your skin is still quite raw in places; legs and thighs.

—Yes, there was a fire after the crash. The flames came almost to my waist.

She put on her large black-frame glasses and asked, in the driest, most clinical tone imaginable:

—And your genitals?

—Um ... no visible damage.

—Come by the hospital tomorrow. I'll give you a very good skin cream.

—Thanks. By the way, this is an odd kind of gym.

—How so?

—There's a bar downstairs by the entrance. With beer, vodka ... even cigarettes.

She sighed.

—It's a Spanish gym. And you, Mr. Byrne, are in Spain.

As I was leaving the gym I saw Ramón Cuevas at the bar, twirling a squash racket.

—Ramón, are you a member?

—Are you crazy? All I've paid for is this racket.

—Can you play?

—Of course not. But it catches the girls' attention when they come down after their showers to get a drink.

He was wearing a smart blue blazer.

—Great jacket, Ramón.

He replied:

—It's not the jacket, it's the hanger.

I got back to my building at the same time as my neighbor, the disgraced general indicted for the attempted coup in February.

—Ah, Mr. Byrne. How opportune to see you. Please accompany me upstairs for a drink. As you may know, tomorrow I begin this charade of a sentence at the military prison.

—I know. I'm so sorry.

—It has no importance. Every Spanish soldier there reveres me. I will suffer no hardship.

I had never been inside any of the other apartments in my building and I realized as I entered the general's that it was twice the size of mine. The reception area was a round room with inlayed wooden floors, busts on pedestals, and large oil paintings on the walls. Beyond that was a vast sitting room with burgundy velvet furniture and long tasseled drapes of green moiré. There were four balconies facing the street, all shuttered. And more oil paintings.

—Please, Mr. Byrne, come in. This is your house. I am glad for the company, as I have sent my wife and daughter to our country place in Segovia to spare them this ignominy. Brandy? I have a splendid old Lepanto.

He poured two generous snifters and we sat down in the dim but regal room.

—*Salud*, Mr. Byrne. And fortitude, to withstand these times of libertines and homosexuals and journalists.

—*Salud*.

He took a long sip of brandy and walked over to a handsome set of bookshelves. He extracted a tome and placed it on the table in front of me. It was the Spanish constitution.

—They accused me of an unconstitutional act. Well, I have read the constitution. How many of the unwashed oafs at my trial have read it?

—You see, Mr. Byrne, Spaniards today want only the facile freedoms; to read a pornographic magazine, to call each other *tú* instead of *usted*. They call that exercising freedom? That is democracy? Hah!—He took another swallow of brandy.

—People today don't know what it means to be a Spaniard; they don't know the history, the idea of Spain. He went to stand beside an enormous oil painting, maybe a Zuloaga, of an imposing woman on horseback.

—That is my wife's grandmother, the Duchess of Medina Sidonia. She came to the aid of Pius the Twelfth during the Second World War, when no other country would help. She subsidized the entire Vatican during the war. She saved the Church! And over here is Vicente Valcárcel Urrutia, my grandfather. He was Franco's envoy to Italy and Germany and three times grandee of Spain. It was he who persuaded Hitler and Mussolini to supply the airplanes to Franco, because he was fluent in Italian and German. He won the war! He saved Spain! But that is a Spain today's people have no idea about—he took another sip of brandy and shook his head—. No, Mr. Byrne, you are not seeing the true Spain. You see the travesty that passes for a bullfight, you eat what the hotel calls a paella and drink what the discotheque says is red wine. But I am from another Spain, the eternal Spain of the olive tree. Do you know that an olive stump can lie unwatered 40 years and still be nurtured back to yield a hundred kilos of fruit? I am from that Spain, *Señor*, hardy and true. Today you go around the country and see castles and convents turned into popular inns and restaurants. And you forget they indeed were castles and convents, fortresses of a culture!

He came to sit beside me on the sofa. And I saw the wounded nobility in his face, the bloodhound eyes.

—What is Spain to people now? A golf player? A singer? A movie actress? Go to the Prado! Look at those men on their horses and on the prows of their ships! Look at those large oil paintings and see why we ruled peoples from the Philippines to Florida; why a Spanish flag on the horizon was an order to kneel! Ah, *Señor*, all that's left of that gleaming age is the varnish on the canvas.

He was quiet for a few seconds, trying to suppress a tear. Then he took a deep breath, raised his glass to me, and said:

—¡*Viva España!*

I raised mine.

—*Viva España.*

The next day I went to Sacred Heart Hospital. I passed by *Doctora* Palomar's office, but she was with a patient. Then I went upstairs to see Claudia Muntaner. As soon as I came into her office she put on the large black-frame glasses that so clashed with her fine face that they began to seem a disguise.

—Hello, Mr. Byrne. I have the skin cream for you. It's organic, no cortisone. It should help.

She had on a cassette player.

—So, you like Paul Simon?

—Well, the middle period, after Garfunkel but before all the ethnic experiments.

—Ah, the *Still Crazy* era.

She permitted herself a twitch of a smile.

—I suppose so. It's refreshing to hear vulnerability in a man.

—Then go to the States. You'll be plenty refreshed.

—Where are you from?

—New York City. And you?

—Barcelona.

—What are you doing in Madrid?

—The medical board assigned me to this hospital; I think just to be perverse.

—May I ask you why you wear those glasses? Surely you could find a more discreet frame. Those remind me of Clark Kent.

She took them off.

—Mr. Byrne, I am a woman, I am short, I am only 29 and I'm a *catalana* in Madrid. There are things I must do here to be taken seriously. I admit some are symbolic.

—What about the Dutch clogs you're wearing? Symbolic?

—No! They're the most therapeutic shoe for your foot. And ... they make me a little taller.

A new Paul Simon song played.

—Do you know this song is about John Lennon?—I asked.

—Really?

—Yes, it was Paul Simon's tribute to Lennon after he was killed.

—Hmmmm. I'm going to hear him tomorrow. Maybe he'll play it.

—Paul Simon's playing in Madrid tomorrow?

—No, in Barcelona. I haven't been back there since I got assigned to Madrid, so I'm taking a brief vacation.

—I haven't been to Barcelona.

She stared at me in disbelief.

—What? Contemporary society, global society, is incomprehensible without Barcelona.

—Well, now that I have the time ...

She fixed her gaze on me and neither of us spoke. Paul Simon lamented *the late great Johnny Ace.*

—I have two tickets for the concert ... if you wish to go.

I didn't know what to say.

—Look, I'll give you a ticket. It's tomorrow at eight in the *Monumental*, that's the main bullring. I'm leaving tonight.

—Are you taking the airport shuttle?

—No. I do not fly. I'm taking the overnight train that leaves from Chamartín at ten—she opened her desk drawer—. Here, take the ticket. Maybe I'll see you there.

She fixed her blue eyes on me.

—In any case, I must tell you: if you do not know Barcelona, you can't know Spain.

I was in a taxi on my way home when I asked the driver to turn around and take me to American Express. There, I booked a compartment on the overnight train and a room at the Hotel Colón, which they recommended. Then I walked to the Hotel Palace for a haircut. In the barber's chair I watched the news along with a few absorbed patrons. The minister of finance had died in a tragic accident at home while cleaning his shotgun. In the stock exchange's first session in days the *peseta* was trading at 189 to the dollar and falling. I called Manola and asked her to pack a shoulder bag for a casual trip. I still hadn't told her I was out of a job; I didn't want her to worry about her pay.

At the hotel bookshop I bought a Michelin Green Guide to Barcelona. I had a few hours to read it so I could appear, if not informed, at least not ignorant. At home I called the kennel and had them come for Pan and Vino. At nine that evening I grabbed the weekend bag Manola prepared and took one more look in the mirror. I decided to shave again.

Chamartín Station was built in the post-war era, when the world's sense of architecture and design went into a coma. Its style is cold and almost soviet in its stubborn ugliness. I got there at nine-thirty and the place was still busy. I looked at the departures board and headed for a bar near the gate. For some reason I was nervous. I ordered a dry martini. And that's when I saw her: in full boots and a white wool sweater, with a small bag slung over her shoulder. I downed my drink and went to meet her.

—What happened to the therapeutic Dutch clogs?—I asked.

—Not for a concert.

—And you travel light.

—Well, I've got plenty of clothes in Barcelona, at my mother's.

—That's handy.

She smiled.

—In Spain you never lose your bed and your closet at your parents' house, no matter how old you are. I understand in the States one is expulsed from the family at 18, as if from a tribe or a herd.

—Well, I was on my own at 20, but that was because my parents had died.

—My mother still keeps my room and does my laundry when I'm there.

The loudspeaker announced the departure of the *Talgo Pendular* to Barcelona. We walked to the gate.

—Oh, I got myself a room for tomorrow night at the Colón. Good hotel?

—Good location, in front of the cathedral.

We boarded the train.

—What compartment do you have?—She asked.

—12 D.

—I'm here, in 9 B. I'm just going to leave my bag and then I'll go to the dining car to get a table for the first seating. Let's meet there.

My compartment was tiny; a single foldout bed hinged to the wall, a washstand and a mirror. But the cot had clean starched sheets and there was a reasonably plump pillow and a blanket in the overhead rack. A flimsy gooseneck lamp with a very dim bulb extended over the bunk. I put my bag in the rack and went looking for the dining car.

It was completely full, with people talking and smoking at the tables and waiters going up and down the aisle. I spotted her at a booth and I made my way there just as the train began rolling out of Madrid.

The table was set with fresh linen and a single rose in a brass vase fixed to the wall. A waiter in a dinner jacket and tie brought a breadbasket and took our drinks order. She ordered sparkling water and I asked for a sherry.

—Trains in the States are nothing like this.

—In Europe we see transport in itself as an opportunity for tourism, not just a means to a destination. Besides, it's ten o'clock; you have to eat somewhere.

The menu offered gazpacho, an omelet, or a salad as first courses. The entrees were roast chicken, steak or sole.

—Wow. In the states they'd have a vending machine.

—Well, that's one reason you're here, isn't it?

A mere ten minutes later we were leaving the clotted confines of Madrid for the groves of Alcalá. The only sound outside the window was the occasional mournful whistle of the train. The only lights came from cottages dotting the landscape.

—Miss Muntaner ...

—Don't call me that. It sounds like you're going to talk about scoliosis. Call me Claudia.

—Okay. I was going to ask you why Madrid is so congested around the city and then so sparsely populated beyond the suburbs.

—Because Madrid is a capital by decree. It didn't grow organically from the needs and like-minded pursuits of people over time. There's no natural reason for it to be there. Those sparse areas like the one we're going through now—that's the way most of Madrid was three or four centuries ago. But tomorrow morning, as we approach Barcelona, you'll see important towns and settlements twenty or thirty miles before we reach the city. There's a reason for Barcelona; it's the culmination, the Zion, for all the surrounding villages. And people are still moving to the center of Barcelona. In Madrid, they're moving out, pushing away from the city with anonymous, identical housing projects, like a mushroom cloud from a bomb.

The conductor came by for our tickets and asked what time we wished to be awakened. Claudia said seven o'clock.

—How will he do that?

—He knocks on your door. Seven's a good time. The train is going along the coast then and the sun is rising. Besides, we can get a table for breakfast. The Spanish passengers won't get up until we reach Barcelona.

The waiter came back. Claudia ordered a salad and the sole. I ordered *gazpacho* and chicken.

—I have to see how the demons he's going to get that soup to the table on a moving train.

—If you drink wine, I suggest Viña Sol, it's a very good *catalán* white.

—Will you share it?

—I don't drink—she looked out the window.

—And you don't fly.

—My father died in a plane crash. He was coming back from a hunting trip in the Pyrenees. So I don't fly. It's more a way to remember him than a phobia.

The waiter appeared at the other end of the car, carrying an enormous tureen with both hands. The train was now rollicking along the creaky track at about forty miles an hour.

—Uh-oh. Here comes my soup. He's got about ten meters to go. I don't think he'll make it.

The waiter then waddled toward us, timing each step to the shifts of the train, which showed either good intuition or long experience.

—The soup man is five meters away … three … two … he's going to make it.

At midnight a waiter announced the second seating. Claudia rose from the table and I slipped a few bills under the check.

—Thanks for dinner—she said.

—For nothing. Thanks for recommending the wine.

We made our way through the cars and reached her compartment.

She took out her key and hesitated.

—Kevin, the girl who was in the car crash with you … I saw her when they brought her in. She was extraordinarily beautiful.

She lay a hand on my arm and said:

—Sleep well.

I tried reading the Michelin but the 15-watt bulb was useless. Besides, my eyes could get no traction on the page because I was thinking of *Doctora* Palomar's comment about being really quite alone. I didn't feel alone or isolated. Why had she said that? I put the book away and turned off the lamp. The train had settled into a steady rhythm and was moving on a straight track. In no time at all I was asleep.

Chapter Seventeen

There was knocking on the door.

—¡Las siete!

I washed my face, brushed my hair, and raised the screen on the window. A golden gleam invaded the compartment. Twenty feet away a long seawall ran parallel to the track. And beyond it, the glassy, placid Mediterranean.

I saw no one on my way to breakfast. I looked through the window in the door to the dining car. At the last table in the corner were the only two people in the car: Claudia Muntaner and a waiter pouring her tea. The woman sitting still, the man slightly bent over her, and the light flooding in from outside, made it a poignant composition. It was almost a Hopper painting.

—Good morning—I said, and sat across from her.

—Good morning. Sleep well?

—Yes. I think the train's sounds and movements actually helped.

She brought the teacup to her lips with both hands. She had pulled her hair all the way back with a headband so it was like a sheaf of new wheat. And I looked at her, really, for the first time: the porcelain oval of her face, the shapely ears, the electric blue eyes, and the fine white skin, flawless even in the streaming daylight.

—This coast is beautiful—I said.

She looked out the window and smiled.

—Yes, it's La Costa Dorada. There are mostly fishing villages along this stretch. Further on there's an artist's colony called Sitges, and then more towns.

—How far are we from Barcelona?

—About an hour. So enjoy the serenity. You won't get any in Barcelona.

The old *Estación de Francia* was a revelation. All the tracks flowed into a soaring terminal with a vaulted ceiling of cantilevered cast-iron girders. And the verdigris on every surface, combined with the steam from the old locomotives and the mistiness of the morning made an anachronistic tableau. It could have been 1910.

—This train station is a wonder. It's like the cathedral of railroads. And that vaulted ceiling; I feel I'm in the ribcage of some gigantic creature.

She smiled.

—I hope they don't tear it down. They've built a new one at Paseo de Gracia, but it's soulless. That's why I wanted to get off here. This is old Barcelona.

Outside, by the taxi stand, was a row of stately palm trees.

—I've never seen palm trees on the mainland.

—Barcelona has its own climate.

We got into a cab.

—*Si es plau, les Rambles.*

I looked at her.

—I speak *catalán* when I'm here. Do you mind?

—Of course not.

The taxi joined the flow of morning rush hour and I noticed at once the difference with Madrid. First the air, moist and coast-like. It was also warmer than Madrid, I guessed by five degrees. But it was the physical presentation of the city itself that surprised me. The apartment houses, the office buildings; even the banks reflected craftsmanship, creativity, even wit.

—Many of them are from our own *Art Nouveau* period. And Barcelona has always been a city of architects.

—Indeed, Gaudí was from Barcelona.

She gave me a hard look.

—Gaudí is Barcelona.

—Claudia, where are we?

We stood on the edge of a broad open plaza ringed by flowing traffic and handsome buildings.

—This is the Plaza de Cataluña. It's the threshold to Las Ramblas, our famous boulevard. Come, it will lead to your hotel. Do you like to walk?

—I'm a New Yorker. We do fifty blocks a day.

It was nine o'clock. Barcelona was busy and eager at an hour when Madrid would be nervous and grumpy.

We began walking down the long pedestrian mall of Las Ramblas. The air was maritime and the boulevard had just been hosed down so the sun turned the puddles into mirrors. I was instantly beguiled by the bazaar that changed from block to ancient block. First were the flower vendors, adorning their storefronts with buckets of roses, lilies, stargazers and tulips. Then came the newsstands, with long tables of books and newspapers in French, Hindi, Arabic, Swahili and Chinese. And it made sense when I saw people walking alongside us in dashikis, dhotis, cheongsams and chadors.

—How far does this go?—I asked.

—All the way down to the sea, to the monument for Columbus. Are you enjoying it?

I stopped in the middle of the boulevard.

—Claudia, I'm enthralled.

She smiled.

—I'm happy you like my city.

I was suddenly aware of a great cacophony.

—What's that?

—The next block is for the bird and parrot vendors.

We walked into the aural bedlam caused by hundreds of cockatoos, parakeets, canaries and macaws.

—Let's turn here, Kevin. I want you to see something. She led me away from the boulevard toward an imposing crested facade clamoring with people going in and out.

—What is it?

—La Bokería.

We went inside and were suddenly in a vast food market; the largest, most tumultuous I had ever seen. Hundreds of stall-keepers were stacking their wares: crates full of strawberries, blushing peaches and shiny limes; pyramids of pomegranates and baskets of dates and figs; dozens of tubs filled with olives and burlap sacks brimming with every imaginable legume, grain and cereal.

—Come over here—said Claudia, leading me by the arm—. This is the seafood section.

Burly men and even some women, all in wader boots, were shoveling shaved ice onto large aluminum trays. Other workers shaped the ice into sloping mounds and artfully placed the fish in descending rows: dark-blue tuna, pink snappers, flat gray soles and spiky orange crabs, slimy baby octopus and shimmering, silvery sardines. There were also baskets of oysters and mussels and scallops and clams; nestled on briny brown seaweed.

—Kevin, look at this.

—Oh my God.

It was a shark, decoratively poised on the chipped ice, with a salmon in its jaws. I turned in place 360 degrees to take in the bustle and hum and the riot of color. If I ignored the stall-keepers' cell phones and the cigarettes dangling from the mouths of their hit-and-run delivery boys, the scene was right out of Brueghel.

—Can we go look at the sea?—I asked Claudia.

—Of course. It's just a minute away.

Las Ramblas had morphed again: Nearing the sea I saw an adult movie house, the Soldiers and Sailors Hotel, and a police station. And on the waterfront itself, the typical flotsam of large port cities: florid streetwalkers, AWOL seamen, skulking drug dealers, and broken drunks.

Claudia must have guessed at my impressions.

—But they'll clean all this up for the Olympic Games.

I turned to face her.

—How?

—They'll give all these people one-way tickets to Madrid.

The Hotel Colón shelters various outdoor cafés on its lee side, all facing the sprawling cathedral. It was Sunday morning, and hundreds of people gathered in the broad sunny plaza, dancing in circles to a mournful, flute-y music. The people, all strangers to each other, joined hands, raised them occasionally in unison, and danced a short back-and-forth jig. All of this was done in utter silence and with no facial expression. Inside each circle was a pile with the coats, jackets and handbags of the participants. People joined circles or withdrew, for no reason I could discern.

—It's *la sardana*, our oldest and most native dance.

—Can you do it?

—Of course. But not in these boots.

I looked at my watch.

—What do you want to do?

—I want to go to my mother's and shower. We can meet for lunch at, say, two-thirty.

—Sure, where?

—Get a cab and tell the driver: Agut d'Avignon.

I raised a forefinger.

—*Si es plau.*

She smiled.

—Very good.

She lingered for a few seconds, gave me a girlish wave, then blended into the crowd.

After checking in and showering, I went back out, just to wander. I was attracted to a side street in the ancient quarter, too narrow for cars. I could almost touch the buildings on both sides if I extended my arms. Very little sunlight trickled down to the mossy cobblestoned pavement and it made the street more of an alley, cool and dim. From any of the ancient buildings I expected a troupe of minstrels to appear at any time. Yet inside the gothic shells of these medieval townhouses were bright new boutiques and art galleries and bars. It was odd to see a somber, gargoyled facade harboring rabidly young people with violet hair and mini-skirts, listening to loud music.

I meandered through the Gothic quarter, stopping in at couple of cafés to soak up the ambiance. I noted at once how the *catalanes* seemed more worldly and urbane. They certainly dressed better. And they weren't as boisterous. Enter any bar in Madrid and you're hit by a wall of sound, uniform and opaque. In Barcelona, I could hear different conversations and the bass and treble of each place.

At two o'clock I debated whether to get a cab or try to find the restaurant on my own. I asked for directions at the hotel and decided I'd walk. I quickly found myself in a warren of narrow, twisting streets and was about to look for a cab when I found Avignon. It was a deserted cul-de-sac. At the end there was a gas coach lamp and a wooden shingle.

The discreet location belied the interior of the restaurant: high vaulted ceilings over elegant tables, impeccable staff moving about quietly, the crackle of a fireplace and the hum of contented conversation. I described Claudia to a woman at the door and she led me to a small alcove, where Claudia sat alone, reading a book.

—Hi—she looked up at me and smiled. A candle on the wall burnished her face.

I sat across from her and was again distracted by her scent.

—What were you reading?

—Deepak Chopra. He's one of my ...

—Gurus?

—I prefer the word guides. His approach is holistic; nutrition plus mental balance and spiritual fulfillment—she smiled—. But don't worry, I won't subject you to any sermons. Still, I brought you some things from an herbalist near my mother's.

She put a small basket on the table with three muslin bags.

—This is chamomile. It's for digestion. This is linden, for your nerves. And this is hawthorn; for heart problems and high blood pressure.

—Which I don't have.

—Yet.

—I'd like a gin and tonic.

—See?

—What?

—You drink in excess. And that, along with the toxins in your diet, will give you trouble later.

A waiter appeared. Claudia ordered Vichy Catalán sparkling water and I defiantly ordered my gin and tonic. Claudia looked sternly at me. I shrugged.

—I can't help it; all my ancestors are Irish.

—All your ancestors are dead.

The waiter brought the drinks and menus. I opened mine.

—Let's see which toxins look good today.

—Well, something healthy that's also very good is *brandada*, a codfish mousse. And, if you must have meat, try the duck with figs. It's very good here.

—Ah! And you know this because ...

—Okay, I used to eat meat.

—Did you ever drink?

—Yes.

—So it's a bit sanctimonious to preach the gospel of Salman Rushdie.

—Deepak Chopra.

—Same guy. Anyway, what will you have?

—Carrot soup and *escaleibada*. It's a local dish.

—Good. I also want a bottle of that Viña Sol I had on the train.

Claudia rolled her eyes.

—Which I'll follow with that whole pouch of hawthorn. How about that?

She laughed and shook her head.

By five o'clock the woody scent of the fireplace had settled over the dining room. I ordered a calvados and Claudia asked for chamomile.

—Tell me, Claudia, which side was your family on during the Civil War?

She looked into her cup.

—They were Loyalists. My grandfather was shot by a Franco firing squad. There are still towns around here that have a 'red' bar and a 'blue' bar. My brother Jordi talks about the Civil War like it was yesterday. But, of course, he's in the Communist Party. By the way, Jordi is having a small dinner tonight at his place, It starts after the concert, if you want to go.

—Sure. But what do we do between now and the concert?

She looked at me for a few seconds.

—Are you religious?

—I like to think I am. I'm a believer, at any rate.

—Then let's go see a church.

The air had cooled and the light was bluer when we stepped outside.

—Are we going to the cathedral?

—No, that's a rambling hodge-podge. I'll take you to a church that's pure Gothic. It's the least ornamental cathedral in Spain, but somehow the most beguiling. It's near the sea and it's called Santa María del Mar.

We entered forbidding wooden doors and were suddenly inside the most soaring spaces I had ever seen in a church; dizzying vaulted ceilings and uncountable pillars. And, all around me, bare walls and sober pews, in the most austere Gothic style. And every ancient stone was air-washed by the sea and the centuries to a monochromatic gray that was almost white. An unseen organ suddenly flooded the cathedral.

I turned to Claudia.

—I'm awed. When was it made?

—Fourteenth century.

—Think of the men then; small, short-lived, prone to illness, and victimized by wars and despots. They still had the sheer faith to <u>do</u> this, to make something holy to match the holiness they somehow managed to find in their existence.

I sat down in one of the pews and, reflexively, knelt facing the altar. I thanked God, as I usually did, for one more day of life and health. I thanked Him for allowing me this trip and for letting me see this church. When I stood up, Claudia was gone. I eventually found her outside, by the sea wall.

—Is that your church?—I asked.

—I don't really have a church. I like many of them, but I'm not a worshiper.

—But you are a Catholic, yes?

—Born one. Right now I'm really more of a pantheist. Most humans cover themselves up with labels and symbols that obscure their elemental selves and it's hard to see what the Creator really had in mind. But plants, animals, the natural world are all as naked today as when God made them. There's no deceit there.

—True. I've never been betrayed by a philodendron.

—You think it's funny?

—Not at all. If I depended on the purity of other humans to sustain my faith, I would have lost it long ago. Your beliefs are as legitimate as any. I just want to know why you have them; what you get from the animals and the forests and the sea.

—What I get is a glimpse into the imagination of God.

She looked at her watch.

—We've got time to see one more thing before the concert.

Fifteen minutes later we were standing in front of *La Sagrada Familia*, the magnificent, joyous and whimsical cathedral unfinished by the master Gaudí. The soaring spires which you see from almost anywhere in the city were like giant rock-candy towers. In fact, the whole façade had a Hansel-and-Gretel quality, though it was nonetheless quite spiritual.

—Do you want to walk to the concert? It's not far.

The idea of a music concert in a bullring was new to me. But, as we approached *La Monumental* with the other 20,000 people going there, it felt quite natural. People were in a festive, but not raucous mood. After all, this was Paul Simon.

We had good seats. Simon stepped onto the stage with an acoustic guitar and wore a baseball cap. He looked small, just a man and his instrument, although there were a half-dozen musicians in the shadows. The air was vibrant and came in fifty-degree wafts from the sea. The stars were out, sharper and more plentiful than in Madrid.

Simon approached the microphone and the entire bullring became hushed.

—*Buona nit*, Barcelona.

The crowd erupted at being greeted in *catalán*.

Simon grinned broadly and began strumming. His back-up singers, three stunning black women, began swaying and oooohing behind him.

—I'd like to ask the audience—continued Simon, strumming a bit louder now—, to hold the hand of the person next to you while I sing this song. It's about determination and fortitude, things the world needs right now and things we can transmit to each other.

I don't think I had actually touched Claudia before that moment and it felt awkward, even if it was Paul Simon asking. But Claudia's hand took mine and I gave in to her warm, strong grasp.

It was a sweet, mellow concert and Simon enhanced the songs with personal narratives. He played old and new material and included the ones Claudia liked best: *Still Crazy After All These Years, Fifty Ways To Leave Your Lover* and *The Boxer*, for which Paul Simon asked us to sing along, and we did.

During the last song, Claudia took my hand again, even though Paul Simon hadn't asked her to.

Chapter Eighteen

If you're ever invited to a dinner party in Spain and arrive to find you're the only American, you'll also find that you are dessert.

Claudia's brother Jordi lived in a vintage apartment in the Gothic quarter. It was another case of someone with a modest occupation living in privileged surroundings, a recurring Spanish phenomenon. Jordi was 35, had studied in Paris, returned to teach high-school French and had decided to run for congress two years earlier. Then he was elected, representing the Communist Party. His live-in companion, Concha, was a blowsy, raven-haired woman of about forty who worked in publishing. Their friend Manolo was a caterer and a flamboyant fifty.

Claudia sat at one end of the table and didn't say much; just smiled at me periodically. I got the impression she was still very much the little sister.

The food was copious and very good, a fish stew called *caldereta*. And the conversation was relaxed. That is, until Claudia cleared the table and brought out a coffee pot and cups. That's when the talk took a shark-like turn.

—So, Kevin—intoned Jordi while he poured himself coffee—. Will you re-elect Bush in November or have you had enough international escapades for a while?

Jordi was a familiar type: a bearded paunchy sort with a twinkling eye and a reservoir of spite.

—I can't predict the mood in the U.S. half a year from now.

—I think Clinton is so appealing—cooed Manolo—. And you can tell he's naughty. The Republicans are all homophobic; too much church.

—If the Democrats win, will they send a career diplomat as ambassador to Spain or just another fund-raising crony?—Asked Jordi.

Concha waved a dismissive hand.

—Oh, you know they won't send anyone of stature. The U.S. only respects countries with oil or money.

I began to sense a pent-up hostility to the U.S., for which I was the lightning rod. And I wasn't sure I'd be able to extricate myself from the conversation gracefully. Claudia looked at me and smiled uneasily.

—And another thing—said Jordi, puffing a Cuban cigar to life—. When will the U.S. abandon the three bases it has on Spanish soil?

—When the Spanish government asks them to—I replied.

Concha leaned in toward me and asked:

—Do you think it's right to have had U.S. troops here for forty years?

—Well, Franco asked Eisenhower to put them here.

—Franco's gone and the U.S. is still here—said Jordi behind a veil of smoke.

—Well—I answered—, we keep sending checks for the rent and you keep cashing them.

Jordi smiled.

—Ah, so <u>we</u> are sending checks?

I had blundered. I had made myself complicit in U.S. policy.

—Well, I meant the U.S. Besides, the bases form part of the NATO infrastructure, of which Spain is a member.

—Ah, a cynical ruse by the government. See how I carefully said <u>the government</u> and not <u>we</u>. We Spaniards always put distance between ourselves and the state.

—But NATO was brought in under the auspices of a socialist government.

—The socialists are dupes, too. If my party had enough seats in congress, we'd leave NATO in 24 hours—boasted Jordi.

—Then make that your party platform in the next election and you might win more than two seats.

There was a momentary lull. Jordi puffed on his cigar, Concha went into the kitchen and Manolo poured himself a brandy.

—Tell me, Kevin—asked Manolo—: is your government actively supporting the gastronomic infiltration of foreign countries?

—The what?

—You know, the fast-food invasion.

—Yes! It's a disgrace—Concha returned to the table with a tray of marzipan and nougat—. There are now fat teenagers in Spain. And I know why the U.S. is doing it. So our young people won't be in shape to fight American soldiers if you invade—she said, with a strong *so, there* nod.

I carefully folded my napkin and placed it next to my plate. I looked at Claudia, who was by now visibly worried.

—I have never heard such an … original theory—I said, as calmly as I could.

—Well, it's not worse than what you've done to the poor Cuban people with the embargo—added Jordi.

—And speaking of the Caribbean, how long will you oppress Puerto Rico? Why don't you make it a state already?

—Because—I said—, the Puerto Ricans keep voting against statehood in every one of their elections. As a state they'd have to pay taxes and I gather they'd rather not.

There was by now a steeliness in my voice that Claudia detected. Her eyes were very alert.

—Another thing—began Jordi's next verbal gambit—: What about the commercial imperialism of your movie industry? Do you deny your government's sponsorship, wanting to brainwash and weaken foreign adolescents throughout the world so they will never rise in opposition to the U.S.?

—I thought we were already doing that with fast food—I replied.

I took a fountain pen from my jacket and wrote in flowing ink on my linen napkin. Then I tossed it toward Jordi, pushed my chair back and stood up.

—That's the name and address of the U.S. Secretary of State in Washington. He's the guy you want. Excuse me.

I walked back to my hotel under the daunting shadows and shapes of the Gothic quarter at two in the morning. I regretted having fallen into the role of apologist for the United States. It wasn't the first time. And it showed the welling resentment of Spaniards—educated, well-traveled, successful ones—toward a society I knew they admired, if grudgingly.

Up in my room I opened the windows and faced the cathedral. It was awash in the glow of half a million bulbs, like a czarist palace at Christmas. I took a cognac from the mini-bar and stood at the window, counting the people—couples and families with children—who were strolling in the square at that hour, on what abnegated Americans would call a 'school night'.

There was a knock at the door.

—¿*Sí?*

—*Soy Claudia*—she whispered.

I opened the door and she rushed at me. She was crying in spasms.

—I'm so sorry, Kevin. I ... it's my fault for taking you there. My brother and Concha, they're <u>so</u> political.

I moved away a bit so she could look up at my face and see I was alright.

She stopped crying and inhaled a sniffle. Her eyes were large and searching.

—Come on in, Claudia. Have a cognac ... oops, forgot you don't drink.

—Well, I could use one—she stepped inside.

I took two small bottles from the bar.

—Come look at the cathedral.

Claudia joined me and there was chilly air wafting into the room. She put her arm inside mine and rubbed her Corinthian head of curls against my chest. And there again was that intoxicating scent. I couldn't resist kissing her forehead and she suddenly arched up on her feet to place her roaming, eager lips on mine.

—*Ay*, Kevin. Are you still glad you're here?

—Here in Barcelona? Yes.

She kissed me again, pressing hard on my lips.

—And here in this room?

I cradled her face in my hands and the glow from outside bathed her radiant, tear-stained cheeks.

—Yes, here in this room.

Then she let loose the bows over her shoulders and her turquoise smock flowed to the ground. She was nude and she pressed herself against me, arching her coltish body. I caressed her arms and her taut round breasts. Then she started unbuttoning my shirt and I loosened my belt. In seconds we were nipping at each other hungrily and lapping at faces and ears and underarms until we fell to the floor and continued there, wrapped in her smock and the hem of the curtains, turning and wrestling in the cathedral's glow. Then she mounted me, pushing down as I pushed further in and she rocked on top of me in hard, short strokes and I just looked up at her and said her name and she looked down at me and her quick blue eyes became urgent and her mouth opened wide and she made a long pleading cry.

Much later she stood by the window, a Maxfield Parrish nymph. I went to her and kissed her head softly.

—What is that scent? It makes me crazy.

—Hmmm? It's called Fracas.

—It's unusual. It smells like …

—Gardenias.

Then it was dawn and I had emptied most of the mini-bar and a very cold mist had moved into the city from the sea.

—I want to go swimming—I declared.

—The hotel doesn't have a pool—said Claudia.

I stood naked on top of a chair and raised my arm like Columbus' statue.

—I mean swimming in the sea!

Claudia shot me a dubious look from the roiled bed.

—You haven't slept. And it's April. The water is freezing.

—I don't care. I have thermal insulation by Remy Martin. Come on, Barcelona is a port; there must be a beach or a cove. Or I can just dive off a dock.

Claudia looked at me.

—Do you have a bathing suit?

—Nooooooo! Of course not. This is a spontaneous … act! Yes, I'm acting … Spanish!

—You're acting crazy.

—Look, Claudia. It's barely seven o'clock. There'll be no one around. I could go swimming in my underwear. Hell, I could go in the water naked!

Claudia stared at me.

—Okay, we'll go. You take one dip in the sea and then you come back and sleep.

I jumped off the chair and lurched toward the bed.

—One dip—I replied solemnly and went toward the bathroom, trying to rectify my walk.

La Barceloneta, the raffish and sometimes dangerous waterfront, was being transformed for the Olympic Games later that year. Claiming that land was needed for sporting venues, the city was razing all the rickety seafood stalls that had given the port its rakish character. Claudia and I found a deserted spit of beach. I took off all my clothes while Claudia looked around for signs of people. Then I waded in. The water was instantly glacial.

—It's cold, isn't it?—Yelled Claudia, hoping to dissuade.

—W-well, at first—I replied, forcing the words out.

I stood still, with the water up to my thighs, knowing I could only withdraw or dive in. Then I rushed at full speed into the lapping, freezing water, expelled all the air inside me and plunged madly into the waves. It felt like a full-body tourniquet. But when I broke the surface I felt only a generalized numbness.

—Hey! I did it!—I yelled to the shore.

Then I plunged in again. And I swam underwater. I could see quite well. Then I floated on the water. I could faintly hear my name being called, but the lapping waves and the cawing gulls were much louder. I went under a few more times and then started heading back to shore, where a very stern Claudia was holding my clothes.

She later told me I had actually been in the water 20 minutes. All I remember after coming out was Claudia stroking me furiously in a cab back to the hotel and then, in my room, when she called for a blanket and another hair dryer. I lay down on the bathroom floor, fortified by a small Kahlúa, and babbled about my «swim».

Claudia was blasting me with two hair dryers, working my body like a Le Mans pit crew.

—You imbecile! You were turning blue!—She screamed.

She wrapped me in a blanket and then continued hosing me with heat.

I'm afraid that I continued to giggle through it all. And I confess that, while she was on the phone to a pharmacy, I took the last bottle from the mini-bar, a Cointreau, and chugged it in the bathroom.

Chapter Nineteen

—Byrne! Where the demons are you?—Screeched the voice on my answering machine—. This is Elena Sotomayor. As they say in America, I've got good news and bad news. I got you an interview for a very good job. But it's not in Spain. Have you ever been to Mexico City? Well, you're going now. Call me, you shameless one!

It was the last day of April. I was back in my apartment listening to messages. Reiko, Ramón and Cottie had called, but not Claudia. She stayed in Barcelona to wait for the train while I took the air shuttle back to Madrid. I called Elena first.

—You scoundrel! Here I am trying to find you a job and you're off on some debauched spree.

—Sorry, an unforeseen trip.

—The best kind! Now listen—her tone turned serious—. You have to be in Mexico City next Monday for an interview. The client is a man who owns a large ad agency there, among many other businesses. He's looking for a manager, preferably from Spain, and the candidate must speak English. The job is big and it pays in dollars. I'll get you tickets for this weekend and I'll send them over by messenger, along with a dossier on the position. And, Kevin, don't screw it up.

I went to Sacred Heart looking for Claudia, but she hadn't arrived yet. For no particular reason I drifted down to *Doctora* Palomar's office. The door was open and she was reading at her desk. I knocked.

—Hello, *Doctora*. You may not remember me.

She tilted her head slightly to one side. She looked handsome and otter-sleek. Again, she wore only one large earring.

—Ah, the peripatetic American orphan. I don't see many. How are you?

I knew that was never a trivial question to a psychiatrist.

—Fine. I may go to Mexico City for a job interview.

—So you would leave us?

—I hope not.

—Then why even go to the interview?

—Because it might seem petulant not to.

—You appear confused. Are you?

—I ... I don't know.

She smiled.

—Well, if you want to talk when you get back, give me a call.

I looked again at the photo of the house in Menorca.

—Do you keep that there to soothe your patients, or yourself?

—Remember, *I* ask the questions. Have a safe trip.—She resumed reading.

Upstairs I met Claudia as she was opening her office.

—Hi, Claudia. Did you arrive this morning?

—Hi. Yes, I just went home to shower and leave my bag before coming here.

—Are you upset because I didn't take the train back with you?

—Yes, I ... was; not so much now.

—I have a job interview on Monday.

Her face brightened.

—That's stupendous! Where?

—Well, Mexico City.

Her whole body seemed to sag.

—But ... how ... would you have to leave Spain?

—I need a job, Claudia.

She gave me a plaintive look.

—Give me your hands.

I did. And she kissed each one. Then she looked up at me with resolute eyes.—Just ... come ... back.

The Aeromexico flight from Madrid to Mexico City takes twelve hours but it gets the trip over with. Other airlines stop in New York or Miami or Dallas, but I didn't want to prolong a journey I wasn't keen to make in the first place. It left me thinking about *Doctora* Palomar's question: Then why even go to the interview? Well, the short answer was that I couldn't reject Elena Sotomayor's effort on my behalf. She might then not be eager to make another one. But there was another reason. As much as I wanted to stay and make my life in Spain, why not take a chance on Mexico? I had never even been there. The job was important and paid well. I had to be open to the possibility of liking it. In essence, I was still only 35 and that was too young to choose comfort over a professional challenge.

Thirty minutes away from Mexico City, I began to see houses on the ground, swaths of low-built dwellings in a tight, vast honeycomb.

—Is there another large city before we reach the capital?—I asked the stewardess.

She looked out the window.

—No, sir. That is the edge of Mexico City.

—You mean it starts 200 miles away? My God. And why are the buildings all so low, just one or two levels?

She looked up and down the aisle and mouthed the word «earthquakes».

The pilot came on and asked us to look out the left of the plane to see the famous volcano. I had an aisle seat on the left side, so I had a pretty good look at it. By the window sat a young Japanese woman absorbed in her book. Suddenly we were flying directly above the mouth of the volcano and the plane lurched violently downward and began rocking hard, the vibrations opening luggage bins and causing bags and packages and food trays to spill onto the floor. The Japanese woman looked out the window, clearly frightened. She screamed in Japanese and looked at me desperately. We were now almost at the level of the crater rim and I began to smell the sulfur. Passengers were pressing their call buttons. Then, just as suddenly, the plane left the crater behind and immediately stabilized. I swore I'd never take another Mexican airline again.

When I landed I was met by a squat indigenous man in a suit and tie. He took my bag.

—Please come with me. *Señor* Jimmy said to take you to the hotel. He will call you there from the ranch.

He led me through the ramshackle terminal out to the curb, where he pointed out a black Lincoln town car with a gold 'V' on the door. He paid off some kids who'd evidently been guarding the car and he opened the back door for me.

The traffic from the airport was sclerotic and the freeway looked quite worn in places. Enormous advertising billboards littered the view along the highway. It seemed they never removed previous ads but simply papered over them sloppily and some large sheets of the new ads had blown away to reveal a palimpsest of images beneath. The buildings all along the highway were mostly two-story structures: gray and soot-streaked, topped with large rusting antennae and lank clotheslines.

But there was something else that permeated everything. It was the air; close, almost clammy, though it wasn't a warm day. It smelled rather mineral and I thought there had been a temperature inversion, because the visibility was no better than 100 feet.

—What's your name, please?

—Benedicto, *Señor*.

—Is there always this much traffic?

He chuckled.

—This is nothing, *Señor*. It's Saturday. Wait until Monday.

—And is this fog habitual in the spring?

He took some seconds to answer.

—Fog? Maybe the *Señor* means the contamination.

I looked out the window at the gray horizon, tinged with yellow.

—How is Madrid now, *Señor*? The Retiro blooms?

—You know Madrid?

—Oh, yes. *Señor* Jimmy sometimes takes me and the other driver, Celestino, so we can take him and *Doña* Laura to the *paradores* and to their house in Marbella.

Nearing what appeared to be the city center, we paused at a rather long stoplight. All at once, the car was accosted by vendors of popcorn, roses, snow cones, roasted ears of corn and even brooms. A thin, shirtless young man, smudged like a coal miner, displayed his gasoline-swallowing, flame-spewing skill. The light changed and they all retreated to the curb to wait for the next red light.

The Camino Real Hotel is a vast complex built in the Mexican-modern style by the great architect Legorreta. It has plazas, staggered terraces, and a vaguely pyramidal structure. But the compelling visual is the vibrant color palette: canary yellow, violet, fuchsia and turquoise, on large, geometric surfaces. Especially against the boxy, monochrome buildings around it, the hotel seemed to proclaim: «Mexico!»

Benedicto took me to the reception desk, where he presented a card with the now-familiar gold 'V'.

—Welcome to the Camino Real, *Señor* Byrne. Any friend of the *Señor* Velasco is an honored guest.

The hotel had many large public areas, done in the same almost-strident colors. I was taken down an interminable hallway by a bellman.

—This hotel is very horizontal.

—Yes, *Señor*. It has only three floors.

I was in a suite overlooking a tranquil garden with a swimming pool and a grove of large banyan trees. I heard a riot of birds but I didn't see any. I showered, dressed and, with my latest book purchase, Robert Hughes' magnificent *Barcelona*, went in search of a cozy chair and a tequila sour. I found a small alcove bar near the entrance and ordered my drink. An attentive waiter brought a silver bowl with toasted corn kernels and a glass of citric-sweet and frothy perfection.

A bellboy passed by, calling out my name. I signaled to him.

—You have a call, *Señor*. He plugged the phone into a wall jack and brought it to me.

—Hello, Kevin! Jimmy Velasco. How was your trip? Are you tired?

—Hi. The trip was fine and I feel surprisingly good.

—Perfect. I'm at the ranch in San Miguel and I know that we'll meet at ten in my office in Mexico City on Monday. But maybe you can come out here and spend tomorrow, Sunday, with us. So we can get acquainted away from the office and the city.

—Sure. How do I get there?

—I'll send the helicopter for you. Can you be ready in, say, an hour?

—Of course.

—Stupendous. Just bring overnight things. We have everything else you'll need. Ask someone at the front desk to show you where the heliport is.

An hour later a white helicopter with gold 'V' livery eased down onto the rooftop of the hotel. *Señor* Velasco was starting to seem like a James Bond villain.

Flying over the massive congestion of Mexico City in a helicopter is like pressing the fast-forward button on a long, bleak movie. But an hour after takeoff I began spying green open land and a sky that was nearly blue. There were large ranch houses and some cattle; even a lake.

—This is the state of Guanajuato, *Señor*. San Miguel de Allende is just a few minutes away.

Below me the land was lush and the air was cool. I took a deep breath. It felt like pure oxygen compared to the brew I'd experienced in the city.

I landed around six in the evening on an emerald lawn in front of an imposing hacienda. The house overlooked a vale that was maybe four miles square. A silvery river snaked across it and horses drank there. In the distance were three brawny mountains, broccoli-green.

I went inside the main house, a three-story manse with an immense atrium in the center. An Arthurian cast-iron chandelier hung down twenty feet above the ample leather sofas and broad mahogany tables. Covering the lacquered wooden floors was the largest Persian rug I'd ever seen, in burgundy and gold. At one end of the room was a walk-in fireplace, blazing away. At the other was an older man in a dinner jacket, standing behind a bar.

A young man in a black suit and a phone cord in his ear approached me.

—Welcome. Your bag has been taken to the tower, where you'll be spending the night. *Señor* Jimmy will be with you shortly. He went riding in the south prairie. Make yourself comfortable. Please excuse me.

I walked over to the bartender, who seemed eager for something to do.

—What's the specialty of the house? I asked.

—Well, *Señor* Jimmy thinks my *micheladas* are good.

—Then I'll have one.

Seeming delighted at my choice, the elegant old man with furrowed nut-like skin began to compose his creation. He took a frosted mug, and turned it upside-down on a dish of salt. Then he put a scoop of shaved ice in the mug, squeezed half a lime into it, poured in almost a whole bottle of ice-crusted Modelo beer and topped the whole frothy, steaming-cold mug with a spoonful of Mexican hot sauce. He handed the brimming mug to me. It looked like a lab experiment.

—Well, here goes—I took two long gulps of the concoction, and the different sensations bloomed in my mouth: the crisp, glacial beer, the tangy lime, the sting of the salt and the burst of the hot sauce—. Wow. I feel like a new man.

The old man beamed and nodded.

—*Señor* Jimmy says this is very good on Sunday mornings.

—I'll bet.

—Hey! Welcome to the ranch. I see Humberto's given you the specialty of the house.

A tall, portly, man in riding boots and a foulard strode toward me, hand extended. I grasped it. I guessed he was in his 50's.

—Jaime Velasco. But everyone calls me Jimmy.

—It's great to be here.

He looked me over for a few seconds, as he might evaluate a horse.

—Very well. Tonight I'm hosting a small dinner in town and tomorrow there's a luncheon here at the ranch, but we'll find time to talk. Why don't you freshen up?

—Casimiro!—He called out. A young groom appeared—. Please show our guest to the tower.

—Kevin, we'll meet back here in, say, thirty minutes?

The tower was a two-story granite building with sentry windows and a conical brass roof. All it needed were gonfalons. The bedroom-in-the-round was sumptuous: thick velvet curtains and a canopied bed, But inside a large mahogany armoire there was a flat-screen TV that swiveled out and a Bose sound system with three rows of CD's. In the lower half was a well-stocked mini-bar. The bathroom had an antique ball-and-claw bathtub and a window that looked out at the sun setting over the mountains. The ledge over the bathtub had a stack of black towels and three glass vases full of hotel and airline soaps: The Ritz Paris, The Dorchester, Singapore Airlines, The Breakers, The Peninsula. It struck me that nothing in that suite even insinuated that I was in Mexico.

Jimmy gave me a quick tour around the main house.

—The swimming pool is actually an underground thermal spring. We just open the lock and the pool fills up with warm mineral water. Over there are the stables. We might go riding tomorrow. The building next to it is the gym. It has Nautilus machines and a steam room, but I haven't used it yet. Oh, and look here at the garage.

There were a dozen stalls in what must have been the original stables. In each stall was a distinctive vehicle.

—I've got a gull-wing Mercedes and a Daimler limo that used to carry Orson Welles around. I like tinkering with them, but who has the time? Okay, let's take a car and head to town.

I followed him to a courtyard where two VW beetles waited with their engines running. The front beetle had men from the ranch. Jimmy opened the door to the one behind. He laughed.

—Oh, these? We can't take vehicles with Mexico City plates down to the village, nor showy cars of any kind, because they'd be vandalized by the locals. So I bought six of these to make discreet forays into town. Nobody bothers with a bug.

The dinner was at the Sierra Nevada, a beautiful Spanish-style hotel in the Relais group.

—Let me show you something.

He led me to a small reading room with a fireplace. On the wall were two vibrant water colors of very Californian swimming pools.

—Are those Hockneys?—I asked.

Jimmy looked at me and blinked.

—You're the first person to notice. My wife Laura is crazy about them and I've tried to buy them a hundred times. But Helmut, the German who owns the hotel, won't sell them to me. I'm tempted to buy the damn hotel just to get the Hockneys.

—What are two Hockneys doing in San Miguel?

—I think Hockney stayed here and gave them to Helmut as a gift.

—If I may say so, they're a little incongruous.

—What? Oh, yes, but I think Laura wants them for our house in Miami. Come, let us go in to dinner.

The group was mixed: a doctor from Monterrey, a stock broker from Zurich, a well-known *telenovela* actress, a Mexican soccer star who had played for Real Madrid, and a venerable Cuban ballet diva. Jimmy asked me to sit beside his wife Laura, a beautiful woman in her early forties with a glowing tan and an Aztec mane of chestnut hair. She was rather made-up, by American standards, but it only enhanced her natural gifts: a large, handsome head, high cheekbones, full lips and large Gypsy-dark eyes. She wore a strapless white gown that set off her bronzed skin and an oval emerald pendant nestled in her cleavage.

—Where in Madrid do you live, Kevin? Her English was fluent but flavorful.

—On the corner of Moreto and Espalter—I answered in Spanish.

—Oh! Behind the museum.

—Yes, on the same street as the church of Los Jerónimos.

—We love that area. Our place is on Claudio Coello.

—That's just a few blocks away.

—Do you go to El Amparo? It's our favorite.

—It's the prettiest restaurant in Madrid.

—And do you know the florist around the corner?

—Castañer?

—Yes!

—I'm there every Saturday.

—Oh, and what's that wonderful fruit and vegetable place?

—Ayala.

—Jimmy!—She called out to the head of the table—. You must hire this man!

In the morning I looked out the top window of the tower and saw servants preparing a very long table out on the lawn, with at least forty place-settings. I took a robe from the closet and went down to do some laps in the thermal-springs pool. It felt like swimming in warm Perrier.

When I came back down after getting dressed, there were already a dozen people with drinks milling around.

—Kevin! Come meet a friend—Jimmy waved me over—. This is Dr. Ernesto Pulido, our ranch veterinarian, the only vet in Mexico with a Bentley. Why don't you two get acquainted?—Then he went off.

I talked with the vet, with a famous Colombian sculptor, with an American golf pro who was designing a course nearby, and with the owner of the L.A. restaurant Ma Maison. I spoke, in fact, to many people. But not one of them was Jimmy Velasco.

By noon there were fifty people standing on the lawn. And the help kept ferrying out trays of *margaritas*, tequila sours, gin and tonics, bloody marys, kirs and, it being Sunday morning, many *micheladas*.

Just then, a bell in the ranch chapel began to peal. Three white peacocks appeared on the lawn, splaying their prismatic panoplies, and they were followed by three *mariachis* in white, silver-chapped *charro* suits. Now, *mariachi* music is not my favorite genre, but these men were extraordinary. They managed to transcend the treacle-y norm of most boleros and delivered the genuine sentiment of the sublime lyrics. And they played all the evergreens: *La Barca, Sin Un Amor, Lo Dudo, Bésame Mucho* and *Perfidia.*

That evening I was taken back to Mexico City in a convoy of minivans. On parting, Jimmy reassured me that we would have a chance to talk in the city. He was staying in San Miguel for an important horse auction, but he promised to call me at the hotel.

The next morning I sat by the pool at the Camino Real, thinking about the surrealism of the trip so far. I had been brought 5,000 miles to talk about a job I still knew nothing about. And my potential employer had proven to be affable, generous and completely elusive. I watched a young Japanese woman swimming laps in the pool and I decided to wait until she finished before I began mine. I'd heard stories of entire pools emptying in Japan whenever a *gaijin* waded in.

It was early, a little past seven. And the garden was already a tumult of bird sounds and shrieks coming from the grove of banyans. But I didn't see any birds. There was one other person by the pool, a tall, leathery-faced man with long white hair, a denim shirt, jeans and cowboy boots. He sipped coffee and puffed on a slim cigarillo. He seemed to be looking at something very far away. Then he turned toward me.

—You American?—He asked in a twang-y voice.

—Yes. How'd you know?

—You just look it, is all. Here on business?

—Well, on a job interview.

He sipped his coffee and smiled.

—I came to Mexico City for an interview, too. In 1960. Been in the country ever since.

—Wow. I guess it worked out, then.

He ground out the cigarillo and looked back at me.

—Son, I'm still asking myself that question.

He saw I was nonplussed and slowly got up and came toward me. He extended a large powerful hand.

—Ben Cooper.

I shook it.

—Kevin Byrne. What business are you in, Mr. Cooper?

—Construction. Been building hotels and casinos all around Mexico for over thirty years—he looked around the garden—. Helped Legorreta build this one, matter of fact.

—It's a striking place.

—Well, this one should last. I know 'cause I inspected every beam and bag of cement that came on-site. And, when the big one hit back in eighty-five, the only things that went down were the two ballroom chandeliers.

—I gather you've been successful.

He sighed.

—Well, I got the damn things built. The methods and the means are another story. But that's Mexico.

—What do you mean?

—I mean if you ever work here, you'll know what needs to be done. But you'll also find out you won't get 'er done unless you unlearn everything you ever knew and learn to do it their way. Problem with that is, you'll get a lot of work here but your skills and your judgement get so screwed up that you won't be fit to work anywhere else. And then, you <u>have</u> to stay.

—Son, let me give you some advice. I don't know what business you're in, but it don't matter. Once you fall for the music and the women and the *micheladas* and the cliff divers at sunset off Acapulco, they got you. And, if you get in the right circles, you'll meet people who'd never look at you back in the States. I danced with Merle Oberon, son, at her house in Acapulco. And I went fishing for marlin off Mazatlán with John Wayne. You know, except for this place, I haven't put up one thing that's been up to code in thirty years. I walked off the Tamarindo job last year. They built that thing out of damn-near balsa wood. And it didn't even take a quake to bring it down, just a tropical storm. A hundred people went down with it, including two little league baseball teams from the States—he became silent.

—Hey, kid, I'm sorry. I just don't know when to shut it.

—That's okay. I think I understand what you were saying. But, well, you can always be proud of this place here.

He looked around.

—Yeah, she'll do.

—By the way, I keep hearing birds within those banyan trees, but I haven't seen any.

He looked at me and smiled.

—So you wanna see the birds? I'll show you the birds.

We walked over to the grove and the bird songs and shrieks were even louder.

He pointed at the high aerial roots and said:

—There are the birds.

—I … I don't see any.

—See those brownish square shapes nestled between branches?

—Yes.

—Those are the loudspeakers. The <u>birds</u> are a recording.

I was dumbfounded.

—Son, if there were <u>ever</u> birds in this place, they died long ago from the altitude or the pollution.

At eleven-thirty I got a call from one of Jimmy's secretaries, telling me a car would pick me up outside the hotel at three. I prepared copies of my résumé, some press clippings about my old agency, a showreel of TV work produced during my tenure, and letters of recommendation from former clients. I put it all in my briefcase. Then I put on my best suit: a black, double-breasted Christian Dior pinstripe, which I wore with a Thomas Pink French-cuff shirt and a Sulka tie.

The agency occupied all four floors of a black granite and smoked glass building on Reforma, the city's signature artery. The entire top floor was Jimmy's suite. Outside his office was an enormous floor-to-ceiling window overlooking Chapultepec Park. Three stunning women sat at their desks, dealing with various undemanding tasks.

When I was ushered into Jimmy's office I found him standing in his underwear and stocking feet on a hassock while two men draped fabrics over his body and marked them with yellow chalk.

—Kevin! Come in, please! Sorry about the spectacle. What I wouldn't give to just go into a store and buy a suit like an ordinary man.

—Hortensio, Fermín, we'll finish the fittings later. Thank you.

The tailors picked up their bolts and measuring tapes and pincushions and left. Jimmy put his clothes back on and led me to a sunken living room. There was a large Rivera painting of a flower vendor on the wall, and an enormous zebra-skin rug.

—Sit, please. Want a drink?

—No, Jimmy. I'm fine.

He poured himself a glass of Krug from a bottle in a standing bucket and sat on a black leather couch across from me.

—Well, Kevin, we finally get to talk. The truth is I need someone to manage this agency—he chuckled—. Because I'm clearly not going to do it.

He took a sip and put his glass on the table.

—Look, Kevin, I'm 52, I have plenty of money and no children to leave it to; my wife wants to travel and I want to go with her—he spread his arms out—. That's all there is to it.

I looked at his face—open, ruddy, frank.

—Kevin, I would give you autonomy. And I'd come by six or seven days a month for consultation, if need be. What do you think?

—Well, Jimmy, that's very flattering, but you don't know my track record or my advertising philosophy or, more importantly, my managerial style.

He came over, sat next to me, and put a hand on my knee.

—I watched you this weekend at the ranch. You're good with people.

Just then, a bell chimed and a female voice said:

—*Señor* Jimmy, the chief of police on line one.

I rose to excuse myself and allow him some privacy.

—No, Kevin, stay. Someday you might be in this situation—he pushed the blinking button on the large console by the couch and spoke into the air.

—Macario, thanks for calling me back.

—What can I do for my friend Jimmy?—Said a warm, avuncular voice.

—Help him, Macario. One of my clients, the advertising manager for Telmex, was kidnapped at an ATM. Young guy, two kids. No word about ransom yet. Can you help, Macario?

—Oooof. Well, if one of my cops grabbed him and he's still okay, he's as good as freed. But if he was taken by some of these new freelancers, I can't help you. Those criminals have just gotten out of hand.

I went back to the hotel feeling puzzled, frustrated and not a little amused. It was preposterous to consider what I'd been through as an interview. It was more like improvised performance art.

I sat by the pool, called for a phone, and asked the operator for a number in Madrid. It was midnight there, but I thought Claudia might still be awake. Then, since I hadn't eaten lunch because I was nervous about the «interview», I ordered a crabmeat salad. A waiter brought it, along with a pepper mill.

—¿*Pimienta?*

—*No, gracias.*

The phone rang. I picked it up and carried it away from the table.

—Claudia?

—¡Kevin! Aaaah, Kevin. How are you? Is it pretty there?

I looked around the garden.

—Well, at this very spot it is kind of pretty. Hey, I didn't wake you up, did I?

—Hah. It's only midnight here. Tell me, have you had the interview yet?

—Um … yeah.

—So tell me! How'd it go?

—It's hard to say.

—Do you know when you're coming back?

—I'm going to try to fly back tonight.

—Wow! So when would you get here?

—Tomorrow evening, if I'm lucky.

—Then be lucky. I really want to see you.

—I want to see you, too. *Un beso.*

—*Otro muy fuerte.*

When I got back to the table I was annoyed to find black specks on my salad.

—*Joven*, I didn't want any pepper on my salad.

—No, *Señor*, I put no pepper on your salad.

That's when I looked at the white tablecloth and the dark flecks falling from the sky.

I didn't want to stay there any longer and asked the concierge to find me a way back to Spain that night. He told me there was an Iberia non-stop that left at midnight and I asked him to get me a seat. Then I wrote a note to Jimmy thanking him for his hospitality and excusing my sudden departure on personal grounds. I put it in an envelope and gave it to the concierge.

—Can you see that this gets to *Señor* Velasco and can you arrange for a hotel car to take me to the airport at ten?

—Of course, *Señor*.

Up in the room I packed my bag hurriedly. I opened a split of champagne from the mini-bar and turned on the radio by the bed. It was playing boleros, but I wasn't in the mood and shut it off. Downstairs, while I waited for the hotel car, I looked up at the sky. There wasn't a single star anywhere; not one. And I concluded that Mexico City had simply fallen out of the whole damn solar system.

My driver pulled up to the curb just as it started to rain. By the time we got on the freeway there was a thunderstorm raging and rain was falling over the windshield in awnings. I leaned over the driver's seat to see what kind of visibility he had. That's when I saw a shirtless man dash out into traffic, trying to get across the six lanes of the freeway. Suddenly I heard a dull crash and tires screeching. In the headlights, I saw the man kneeling in the highway, drenched and bleeding. A sudden flash of lightning illuminated him. I assumed then that traffic would stop completely, when a second car hit him. Then a third.

When I got to the airport the storm had passed but the terminal floor was soaked and the air smelled dank and loamy. I went upstairs to the Iberia lounge and had two quick vodkas. The ambience in the lounge was rather festive; about twenty Spaniards waiting for the Madrid flight were listening while two others sang and played guitars.

—Hey!—One of them called out to me—. Are you on the Madrid?

—Yes, I am.

—Well, what are you doing over there? Bring us some champagne from the bar and get over here. We need a better singer.

I joined my dear, irrepressible Spaniards for Bosé's *Te Amaré* and Victor and Ana's *La Puerta de Alcalá*. Then I heard them call our flight.

—Aw, don't worry about that. They're not going to leave twenty of us here.

I managed to persuade the group that "they" just might do that and we began to waddle toward the gate, another contingent of the gregarious and emotive Spanish colony. One of the guitarists, an endearing and woozy 22-year-old named Javier, asked me whether I was returning to Madrid for *las fiestas*. That's when it struck me. It was May tenth. It was the beginning of the two-week festival of San Isidro, Madrid's patron saint. No wonder there were so many Spaniards going back. And their mood confirmed that there is no expatriate more homesick than a Spaniard.

My young guitarist friend sidled up to me.

—Have you ever taken this flight before, man?

—No.

—It's the best. It has tremendous *ambiente*. Last year when I took it I only sat down twice in twelve hours: once for takeoff, and once to vomit.

Chapter Twenty

I sat back in the taxi, exhausted but happy, gliding down Serrano to my place on a blue-mauve evening in May. At a stoplight I saw a billboard for Bacardi rum. The visual was a strobing image of beautiful young people in a disco. The headline was: *Sleep when you're dead.*

I was home.

On my answering machine I had messages from Cottie and Ramón. They both wished me luck in the interview. It was seven o'clock. I called Claudia at the hospital.

—Are you here already?—She asked.

—Yes, I'm home.

—Are you absolutely worn out from the trip or could I see you for a little while? I get off at eight.

—Sure. I think a shower and clean clothes will invigorate me. I've just flown twelve hours with a group of your most omnivorous, omnibibulous compatriots and I could use a scrubbing. I wonder how they'll clean the plane. Do you want to meet at Bar Hispano at, say, eight-thirty?

—But that won't give me time to go home and get cleaned up for you.

—Like I care.

When I got to Bar Hispano it was agreeably full of the smart-looking Spanish professionals who go there. I ordered a dry martini, and listened to Juan Luis Guerra's mellifluous *Burbujas de Amor.* At a quarter to nine Claudia came in and hurried over to me. We hugged and then held each other with a long kiss.

—God, I missed that smell. Hey, your hair's wet. Is it raining?

—No. I just got out of the shower at the hospital.

—Let me take your coat off.

—No! I can't.

—Why? What's wrong?

—Look—she folded back the hem of her coat to reveal a baggy green pant leg.

—What are you wearing?

—Surgical scrubs. I didn't have any clean clothes to change into.

I laughed out loud.

—Take your coat off, I'll borrow a knife from the bartender, and you can go around the bar like you're going to perform surgery.

—Shhhh, you idiot.

The song playing then was *La Lambada*, that infectious *vallenato* piece that had overrun Europe the year before.

—Do you want to get some dinner and then go dancing?

—What?!? In this outfit? Besides, you might feel fine now but you could collapse any minute. And I have to teach my juvenile gymnastics class first thing in the morning. Let's just get something at the bar and go back to your place.

—Sounds like a plan—and we kissed again.

In the morning I walked Claudia to the school where she gave a weekly class to a group of twelve-year-olds. She introduced me as a friend from *"América"* and asked me to talk a bit about school in the States for kids their age. I told them that I was terrible in math and science but discovered that the girls all took French and Spanish, so I signed up for all the languages the school offered. There were titters. Then I said that I began Spanish when I was twelve and I explained what a language lab was. They were fascinated. Then I asked for questions and one boy wanted to know if there was anything about school that I hated when I was their age. I said yes. It was gym. They laughed uproariously. I looked over at Claudia. She was smiling.

That afternoon I met Reiko for a walk in the park. We went by the spot near the boat pond where the Russians used to sell their trinkets and sing their dirge-y songs. But there were no Russians now. Vassily had been found dead, murdered, just a few weeks earlier. And it had been the sinister Mr. Bill Ellis who had come to give her the news. But he apparently didn't just want to share her grief.

—He say he need Vassiry things; crothes, book, retter. But I say no. Then he say he give me money. I stirr say no. Then he make very bad face and say I can be ... how you say ...

—Deported?

—Yes.

I knew he could probably arrange that.

—Did he say who killed Vassily?

—Yes. It was KGB. They put poison inside.—Then she broke down and began sobbing. I held her to my chest.

—Go ahead. It's okay to cry.

A few minutes later she was her usual, serene self.

—First I think I reave when Vassiry die. Then I think no. It is winter and winter make it more bad. I say, Reiko, wait for spling. Spling make it more good again. But here is spling and Reiko no more good again. Maybe no more good never.

We walked to her metro station.

—I think I go back to Japan. Not very interesting, Japan. But not so dangerous. I going to miss you, Kevin. I rike you and Vassiry orso rike you. I hope you good ruck.

I kissed her on the forehead and watched her walk away, the saddest woman ever to wear a white vinyl miniskirt and tangerine lip-gloss.

When I got home I had two messages, one from Claudia and one from Elena Sotomayor. I called Claudia.

—Hey! Guess what? The kids today told their teacher about you and she suggested you come back and the give all the students a little presentation on American schools.

—Claudia, I know nothing of the subject.

—Just talk about your own experience.

—My experience at their age is twenty years out of date.

—It doesn't matter. These kids are starved for a taste of America. They're tantalized by the movies and the music, but they want to know what life in the States is like for kids like them. Please come talk to them. Just thirty minutes.

I agreed to go the following day. Then I called Elena.

—Evil one! Why didn't you call me from Mexico? I had to wait to hear it from my client!

—Jimmy called you?

—Well, not personally. A secretary called saying the *Señor* Velasco wants you in Mexico City no later than June fifteenth because he leaves for one month on safari the following day. They're sending a contract by DHL. So you did it! You got the job!

—Uh, well, I need to talk to you about that, but not now.

The next morning I reappeared at the playground of the school in the El Viso neighborhood. Almost 100 students, the entire school, were gathered there. A portly woman in her sixties gave me a warm introduction. We had never met. I then spoke extemporaneously about the life of a twelve-year-old in the States: the sleepover parties, the chaperoned dances, the class trips to Washington D.C. or a Broadway show. I didn't talk about growing pains, mean-spirited classmates, social inadequacies, and sheer alienation. The kids listened politely until I came to the subject of the weekly allowance. This last concept proved as foreign to them as it was riveting; the idea of a stipend for chores—that boys would get money for mowing the lawn and girls would be paid for washing the car. When I saw how preteen capitalism had caught their attention, I felt like an instigator of subversion. Claudia just grinned from the sidelines.

—You were wonderful! Those kids are at an awkward, skeptical age. And you engaged them. You really should consider it.

—Consider what?

—Teaching.

I laughed derisively.

—Claudia, you'll notice I have no kids, I never talk about kids, I don't want kids. I'll never even have nieces and nephews.

—But you commanded their attention.

—Only because they knew that, the second I shut up, they could all go to lunch.

—Kevin, if you began teaching kids, it would be ... like a second child-hood.

—But I didn't like my <u>first</u> one!

—But think of those eager minds, sponges for knowledge.

—Hah! The boys all wanted to know about Michael Jordan and the girls about Madonna. That's a big maturity gap and doesn't bode well for any marriages within this group.

—Kevin, I'm saying that you can communicate with them. You're cred-ible to them. And that's a gift.

—Maybe it's all those years of presenting to infantile clients.

Later that day I finally connected with Cottie at Galería. I hadn't been there in a few weeks and the place was a sight: most of the boutiques were closed, the escalators were immobilized and the whole second floor was dark. I took a table in the still-open café under the rotunda. The single for-lorn waiter came over, his footsteps echoing in the room.

—I'm waiting for a friend.

—You should order soon. We close now at six.

—Then let me have a bottle of Freixenet and two glasses.

Cottie walked in; tall, rangy, handsome. He looked like a first baseman manqué.

—Hey, *Kemo Sabe*. Why all the empty tables? Was it something you said?—He poured himself some champagne—. How was *Le Mexique*?

—*Épouvantable.*

—That good, eh? *Salud.*

—*Salud.*

We drank and I told him about my visit to the middle school and Clau-dia's suggestion that I turn to teaching. His sudden laughter exploded in the empty café.

—Teaching? If you start living on a teacher's salary, then you have bought your last pair of Gucci loafers, *caro mio*.

We talked for a while until there was silence. Then Cottie spoke abruptly.

—There's something I gotta tell you. Kelly's being re-assigned ... to the NATO desk in Frankfurt.

My stomach tightened. I took a long drink of champagne.

—I take it you're thinking of going with her?

—You take it right. Yeah, I'm leaving with her.

I looked around the ghostly Galería.

—When?

—Oh, don't worry; not for a week or two.

—Good. Then we'll have time to see each other.

—Bags of time! Time enough to get sick of each other, *Braumeister.*

We were both quiet for a minute.

—Oh! I almost forgot. I want you to have something.

He reached into his shoulder bag and took out a thick sheaf of papers bound with large clips.

—It's a copy of my manuscript. It's not finished yet because I don't know the ending. Nobody knows the ending.

In all the years we'd been in Spain, he'd never shown me a single page of it. I took the manuscript, about 400 typewritten pages. I looked at the cover:

The Same Love Twice
A novel by Cottard Chubb

He stood up.

—Maybe I'll find the ending in Germany. Anyway, you can read it sometime when you're bored. After all, you're in it—he smiled sheepishly—. Your character's name is Julian. Is that too fey?—He drained his champagne glass and hoisted his shoulder bag—. At any rate, you're in all the good scenes ... all the best scenes.

We looked at each other for a few seconds.

—Well, hey, gotta go!—He exclaimed, a little too cheerfully—. But there's still plenty of time to get together.

—Plenty—I said.

We were still looking at each other. He spoke:

—Take it easy, Butch.

—You too, Sundance.

Then he walked out of Galería into the mild May evening. And I never saw him again.

Chapter Twenty-One

I wanted to tell Claudia about Reiko and Cottie leaving. But I didn't get the chance. She had left me a message:

—Kevin, guess what? I'm going to a physical therapy seminar in Valencia. I'll be back Monday. I'm so excited about it and the hospital's paying for everything! I'm leaving for the train station right now. Can you take care of yourself for three days? *Besos.*

I sat in my apartment for an hour, just thinking. My dogs sensed a ruminant mood and huddled next to my armchair. With Cottie leaving, I would become the last expatriate from that first summer, back in '84. No more Piet and Friedlander. No more Randy and Joel. No more Barbara, no more Reiko. No more Simone. *Doctora* Palomar's words now bloomed with meaning:

—So you are now really quite alone.

Except that, when she said them, she meant family. And, when I heard them, I had friends. But, damn it, I thought, slapping the armrest and startling the dogs, I am not alone. At least, I thought, I have Claudia. Even though she was also away.

I felt uneasy. I'd always been a person who 'made his own dinner and cleaned his own plate'. And now, I was experiencing a sudden need for ... others.

I needed to think; maybe to go away, too, until Claudia came back. And there were practical matters: Elena Sotomayor needed an answer. And I had to resolve my status in Spain. I decided to leave Madrid for a few days; in fact, leave the peninsula. The next morning, a Friday, I went to American Express and got plane tickets to Menorca. And I had them book me a hotel near the town of Horizonte.

From the air Menorca looks a little like a boomerang. It's a primitive, wind-swept island with few year-round inhabitants. It's surrounded by jewel-like seas that lap at its craggy coast. I was staying at the Trafalgar Hotel, which seemed an odd name until I was told Menorca had actually been British for a few decades. I stowed my bag and walked off to find the village of Horizonte.

It wasn't far, about ten minutes down the road. It was a series of white-washed cottages nestled behind wind-bent trees. I walked along Avenida del Campo, the only road. One of the cottages had a rusting hulk of a car in front. The wreck had been there so long that vegetation was slowly engulf-ing it. Six scruffy cats scampered down to inspect me. Up a mossy mound of lawn was a woman in an orange robe, clearing brush away from the cot-tage. She was corpulent, with long straw-like hair and a raw, reddish face. She reminded me of Rodin's Balzac. She tugged noisily at the dry branches and weeds until she noticed me.

—Acchh … I didn't hear you.

She came down three granite steps, with difficulty, to where I was. There was something sylvan about her, like a female Merlin. She looked about 50, with florid, weather-beaten features and very knowing gray eyes. She looked closely at me.

—You are a stranger, yes?—She turned to the cats—. What do we think about this stranger, eh?

She was definitely not a Spaniard. I thought she might be Dutch, from her twisted syntax and impressionistic pronunciation. She turned her watery eyes and sun-spanked face on me.

—I think he is just lost. Are you lost?

—Well, I'm looking for a house.

—Acch, You want to rent for the summer?

—No. I'm looking for a house I saw in a photo. This is Horizonte, yes?

—Yes, like the novel … Lost Horizon.

I stared at her. She had just named my favorite book from high school.

She turned back to the cats that were licking in vain at the empty cans that littered the ground.

—Oh, I think this stranger knows this novel.

—The house I'm looking for is white, with two chimneys and a large bougainvillea in front. I think there may be a small swimming pool, too.

—Acch, that is Papallona. *La Doctora* Rosa have this house—she stared at me—. You need to consult *la Doctora?*—She leaned in closer—. You don't look crazy.

—No. I just wanted to see it, since I happen to be in Menorca.

—It's up the road, the last house on the right.

—Thank you. I'm sorry for taking up your time.

—Acch—she lifted a meaty arm—. Suffer no sorrow.

I found the house right away. The gate was open and I looked at the familiar image: the storybook white house with soft contours, the two chimneys, the clay-tile roofs, the small pool, embraced on all sides by crimson bougainvillea bushes. It looked like a large, softening cream cheese surrounded by raspberries. There was a winding path from the gate that skirted a large willow tree. At a round table by the pool, reading a book in her bathing suit, was *Doctora* Rosa Palomar. She looked up.

—Come closer.

I approached her.

—What are you doing here?—She asked, with a hand shading her face.

—Well, I was in Menorca.

—No. I asked what are you doing <u>here</u>.

I took a few seconds to say:

—I don't know.

She put her book face down on the table and sighed.

—Sit down and let me tell you.

I took a chair and she leaned in toward me.

—You are a confused person. First, you have not really recovered from your accident. Secondly, you are still hurting from the loss of your job. And now, something else is going on in your life, perhaps yet another loss, and you don't know how to go forward.

—I ... maybe I do need to consult you ... professionally.

—Maybe. But this is the most unprofessional way to do it. Call my office in Madrid and make an appointment.

—You're right. And I'm truly sorry. I can't expect to fix anything with five minutes of free advice.

I looked at the book on the table. It was *Out of Africa*.

—Hmmm, Isak Dinesen. I love that book.

—I like women who've faced adversity. Dinesen had a brutal, pitiless experience in Africa, but what came out of the crucible is this beautiful, lyrical story. Not many people can perform that kind of alchemy.

She looked at her watch.

—It's lunchtime. You can come with me, if you like. There's a place down in the village, right on the water.

—I'd like that very much.

She put on a white robe, which set off her rich tan. It had a cowl and her close-cropped head against it made her look like a Star Wars queen.

Down in the village we sat at a small place called *El Trébol*. It was freshly whitewashed and had dark green shutters, what seemed to be the visual leitmotif of the island. A fishing smack put-putted up to the dock of the restaurant and two men got out. They went inside lugging a copious catch in mesh bags that were hemorrhaging seawater. A few minutes later a waiter came out and wrote on a blackboard everything we had just seen brought in from the boat.

We ordered a shellfish stew and a bottle of Viña Sol. She listened while I told her how all my friends in Spain were leaving, one by one.

—For me, it's been a bit traumatic.

She waited a second before exclaiming:

—Nonsense! For you, it's merely inconvenient. For years you have floated on a raft of friends who were always available when you didn't want to be alone. Now the raft is gone and you have to swim. Now you're alone. And it's an inconvenience, which you hate. Also, you have been able to spend your way into a mild stupor with nice things, fine clothes, good food. Now you're out of work, another inconvenience. But don't you dare call it traumatic. For you, it's merely the discontinuation of your pleasant sleepwalk through Spain.

I took a minute to digest all that.

Then I told her about my experience in Mexico and that I needed to make a decision.

—Well, if it pays well, you can resume your very convenient lifestyle. Over there.

—But I don't want to go.

—Then don't.

—But I need a job.

—Why? What for? You have no immediate need, no dependents, no psychological need for a job to validate you or raise your self-esteem because you already think rather highly of yourself. No, you want a job to keep your <u>lifestyle</u> and thus not have to examine your <u>life</u>. The job you claim to need is really the money to continue this agreeable sedation that keeps you from having to look at things too closely. But someday, you'll face a choice. As they say in the U.S., your money or your life.

She took a sip of wine and sat back in her chair.

—How old are you?

—Thirty-five.

—And how long do you think you'll get by on looks and insouciance?

—I've never done that.

—HAH! Of course you have! And it works, so far. Tell me, what would you like written on your tombstone?

I thought for a minute. It was a good question.

—Got it: Kevin Byrne, mourned by florists, concierges and *maitres d'* ... worldwide.

She smiled.

—And you're not insouciant? But I've got one that's shorter and more apt: "Kevin Byrne: women liked him".

An hour later we were walking along a promontory above the village.

—Right now, Kevin, you have no obligations. You have unconfined potential. But that's the problem. You see, you are now like a mass of dough rolled out across a surface. You have the potential to become, say, six croissants or sixteen buns or sixty cookies. But without definition, without cutting up the dough to give it form, you remain everything potentially, but nothing in actuality. In short, the obligations that limit our acts also give us shape; they help define us.

—So you're saying I need a cookie cutter?

She laughed.

—Well, yes. Something that sets limits for you but at the same time shapes your identity.

She took me down a path that led to a scallop of a beach down below.

—Come. I want you to try something.

We arrived at a sparkling cove of blue and green water. Above it was a slope of pure chocolate-y mud, bare of all vegetation. Also bare, much to my unease, were the six people lying there. And they were entirely slathered in mud, including hair and genitals. They looked like yule-log cakes. *Doctora* Palomar began to strip. She had a large firm body with heavy breasts and no pubic hair at all.

—You need to coat every part of your body to get the full effect. Come on, take your clothes off.

I began, slowly, to disrobe. Then I knelt down gingerly on the mud and began to coat my arms and then my legs.

—Not like that, silly. Here, like this—she was scooping up mud with both hands and slapping it onto my head and down my back. Now do it like me—. And don't forget to do your genitals and your rear.

A couple of the others lying there sat up and observed me. I had no choice. In a minute I was completely covered and actually would have liked to look in a mirror to see if I was like one of those Irving Penn tribesmen.

—Very well, now lie in the sun for thirty minutes on each side.

—Are you sure I won't end up with things sprouting from me or turn into a piece of terra cotta?

—No. Afterwards you dive into the sea and it all comes off. And what comes over you is a sense of general well-being.

I think I may have dozed off until a resounding splash awoke me. The *doctora* had plunged into the sea. She called out forty feet from the shore.

—Come! Dive in!

I did and then I saw the trail of mud I left in the pristine water become a comet's tail that slowly settled on the rippled seabed.

Later we were drying ourselves off just as the sun was setting. We were the last two people left in the cove. She toweled herself slowly, sensuously. And she looked simply voluptuous. Suddenly she stopped drying herself and looked down at me.

—Are you thinking of making love to me?

—What? Uh … no! Of course not.

—Yes, you are. And do you know why? You were in the eighth grade when your mother died, yes?

—Yes.

—And you loved her?

—Very much.

—And how old was she when she died, leaving you forever?

—Forty-six.

—Exactly my age. Let's get dressed.

We walked back to her house and she stopped at the gate. She stroked my cheek with the back of her hand.

—Kevin, you need to be inconvenienced, challenged. You need to face adversity, for that is the only way you'll shed the armor that protects your heart. Otherwise you may never find a purpose. And that is what you need: a purpose.

The next morning, a Sunday, I walked on a bluff above the roiling sea. The light was pearly, the wind stiff. It reminded me, oddly, of the coast of Cornwall. Maybe that's why the English had been drawn here and why they still came in the summer. I passed by a British-style pub on the way to my hotel. There was a banner outside advertising the Manchester-Arsenal game on cable TV. I went in for a beer and saw some very tattooed Brits grimly determined to have a good time. That evening I flew back to Madrid and landed in the city under a recumbent moorish moon.

When I walked into my apartment I saw a DHL envelope on the floor. I knew what was inside: the contract from the agency in Mexico City; the contract I was never going to sign.

—Are you crazy?

Elena Sotomayor sat on the edge of her desk and looked down at me.

—I'm sorry, Elena. I cannot take that job. There'll be others. Maybe for less money, maybe in a small agency or a smaller market.

—I don't think you fully appreciate your prospects in the advertising field. First, you can forget about Spain. You're tainted here. And don't even dream about going back to New York. You've been away for years and, in that time, advertising has evolved into a game you wouldn't begin to recognize. Your only hope is somewhere new.

—Fine. Just not Mexico City.

—Why not?

—Have you been there? Not even <u>Dante</u> could conjure up Mexico City.

She sighed.

—The job in Mexico City could be a steppingstone to something in Latin America. Or something in the U.S., in Texas or California. At the very least, it's your professional redemption; a lifeline. And, Kevin, with your lifestyle, I don't know how long you can stay out of work.

—Well, as someone recently told me: your money or your life. Maybe I have to rethink some things. The only thing I'm sure about is that I want to stay in Spain.

—Then you'll have to re-invent yourself.

—But advertising is all I know how to do.

—Nonsense. None of us knows what he is truly capable of. Maybe this crossroads will lead you to discover a whole new career.

I stood up and extended my hand.

—I'm sorry about this, Elena. I know you sold your client on me.

She shook my hand.

—Don't disappear, Kevin. I want to know what happens to you.

Outside on the Castellana, Madrid's main artery, it was just another Monday morning. Traffic was heavy, people walked in small groups to their favorite cafés, the parks staff were watering the flower beds, and nannies were pushing their strollers. And nobody could have cared less that one person in the picture had perhaps suffered a grave blow. It reminded me of that mural with Icarus plummeting toward the sea because he flew too close to the sun and the wax on his wings melted. Well, Icarus' plunge is a tiny detail of the painting, an incidental figure against the enormous image of a teeming city. There I was, taking a professional header into my own private Aegean and nobody noticed.

I began walking to Turner's bookstore. I had finally concluded that I'd need to get a cheaper apartment and I was going to leave a note on their bulletin board. On the way, I began wondering whether I'd ever work in advertising again and whether that was truly important to me. I knew, I was certain, that I was still good at it. But did that matter? Maybe I could persist, desperately, to stay in the business in some capacity. Or was it futile?

Maybe things had already been determined and, simply, the only one who didn't know it was I.

I then wondered whether Elena was right about my not being able to re-enter the New York orbit. If so, it hurt my professional pride a little, but it didn't change my status as a native son. I knew I would always carry the imprint of The City, the place that made me, as Sonia once said. Besides, I had another place now. I had Spain. And I wasn't here because I'd become deracinated. I was no refugee; I would always be a New Yorker. But I would also, always, feel like a Spaniard.

On my way home I bought the latest issue of *Anuncios*, the advertising trade weekly, out of habit. My old agency appeared on the front page. Its acting director announced the layoffs of 80 percent of the staff, due to 'unfavorable economic conditions and currency exchange issues'. A week earlier the Spanish government had suspended all state-funded advertising. When asked if the Madrid office might close, Todd Bienbach called that a remote possibility and pointed out that any remaining clients could still be serviced from the office in Lisbon. I felt badly for the people, the Spaniards, who'd be hurt by this.

Back in my apartment I had a message from Claudia. She was back from her seminar in Valencia and wanted to come over after work. I was about to call her when the phone rang.

—Is this Kevin?—Asked a plummy female voice.

—Yes.

—Hi! It's Sloane Endicott!

—I'm sorry?

—Sloane Endicott. We were at Bryn Mawr together. I was a friend of Laura Cabot's, the girl you were sleeping with junior year. You <u>do</u> remember her, don't you?

—Yes, I … of course I do. How'd you find me?

—The alumni directory. Actually, I'm here in Madrid and I was wondering if you wanted to meet for a drink.

—Um … yeah, I guess so.

—Whoa! Try to rein in your zeal! I'm at the Palace Hotel. Is that handy?

—Quite. I'll see you there in thirty minutes.

I took the dogs for a walk and tried to recall her. I remembered a tall, gangly girl from Connecticut who wore pearls to class and mailed her dirty laundry home to be cleaned.

The Palace was quiet and I spotted her at once.

—Hiiiiiii!—She got up and spread her arms wide—. It's two kisses here, right?

—Yes, two.

We switch-kissed and sat down.

—Well, look at you! Mister Spain!

—You look well, Sloane. Tell me, how's Laura?

—Divorced! But aren't we all?

—I'm not. I'm not even married.

She gave me a sly look.

—Well, you always were a little slippery.

A waiter appeared.

—Can they make a martini here?

—A great one.

—That's what I want.

—*Dos, por favor.*

—So! Tell me what you do in exile. I never figured you for a fugitive. Have you found 'what you were looking for'?—She asked in a mock lofty tone.

—Yes. I found Spain.

The waiter brought our drinks and she downed half of hers in one gulp.

—Hmmmm. This is yummy. So, tell me: what's life like here? What does an American do? I mean, once you go to the Prado and you see a bull-fight and you eat the suckling pig or whatever, how do you actually live here?

—Quite well, really.

—What about a social life? Do you know other Americans?

—I know people from all over.

—Waiter!—She called out—I'm getting another one. Ready for another?

—I'm fine, thanks.

It didn't take long to exhaust our reservoir of small talk. Finally, she said:

—You know, we haven't seen each other in fifteen years.

—Sounds accurate.

—How do I look to you?—She asked, blinking several times.

—Pretty much the same.

Except I didn't remember her being thin and fidgety. Nor the tiny lines at the corners of her mouth. She took out a cigarette.

—Can I smoke here?

—You're in Spain. You can smoke in church.

She lit up quickly and looked at me.

—You've changed so much, Kevin. Now you dress in earth tones. And you wear suede and cashmere. And I bet whole days go by that you don't speak any English.

—Weeks, probably.

She put out her cigarette impatiently. The waiter brought her another martini.

—So you've really gone native.

—Well, I've been here a few years.

—Tell me, what is it about Spanish women?—She leaned in closer—. Do they have a hell of a wiggle?

She sat back in the chair, and asked:

—You're out of the pool, aren't you?

—I don't know what you mean.

—I mean that you're out of circulation, as far as American women are concerned. Am I right? I mean, have you gone out with a single American woman since you've been here?

—No.

—Would you even consider dating an American woman again?

I left her fifteen minutes later, having received my periodic inoculation against brittle, aggressive American womanhood.

On my way home I passed by the church of Los Jerónimos. The priest, Father León, was at the entrance.

—Excuse me, do you have a minute?

—Of course, Father.

—I am being re-assigned next week, to the provinces.

—I'm sorry to hear that.

He smiled.

—I serve the Lord wherever I'm sent. Besides, I'm from a small town in Alicante. Madrid is too much city for me. But I wanted to tell you about my replacement; a young priest from Ireland named Father Patrick. He speaks Spanish fluently, but he asked me about the possibility of a weekly mass for English-speaking Catholics.

—That's a great idea.

—Would you be able to help?

—Sure. I can leave an announcement at the embassies: U.S., U.K., Canada, Australia, New Zealand, South Africa, Ireland. I think you'd get a good crowd.

—Stupendous. Of course, we'd also need English-speaking lectors to do the two readings after the Gospel. Could we count on you?

I thought about that.

—Of course you can.

Claudia came over about eight. I was busy in the kitchen, making stock from the remains of three roast chickens I had in the freezer.

Claudia made a face as she glanced tentatively into the bubbling pot.

—How can you keep those ... carcasses in your home?

—Oh, come on, admit <u>these</u> toxins smell pretty good.

—Kevin, I have an idea.

—What?

—Let's go for a walk.

—O-kay—I said, warily—. Let me turn the stove off.

We were out in the mild evening, drinking from the sweet pool of late May. Many people were only just leaving work, thanks to the bizarre Spanish schedule, so the streets were alive with people strolling and doing some shopping before the stores closed at nine.

—Kevin, I know of something you could do that would be perfect. Remember the kids you spoke to?

—Sure.

—Well, theirs is a public school with few resources. They don't even have gym class, which is why I go one day a week. But another thing they don't have ... is an English teacher.

I stopped suddenly.

—Claudia, what are you thinking?

—Kevin, you could help them learn English, so when they finish high school, they can apply to university. Right now they don't have a chance against the kids from private schools who take English classes every day and probably spend their summers in England or Canada. Kevin, they would have a chance!

—Claudia, that's preposterous. I'm not a teacher, I'm not trained.

—Kevin, promise me you'll speak to the school director about it. Please?

We were out on Serrano, the Rodeo Drive of Madrid. The Mallorca café was on the corner.

—Claudia, let's just go have a drink.

We went into the café, full of older women with cotton-candy hair and furs, picking up their boxes of pastries. I ordered champagne.

—Claudia, it's a noble notion. And I think it would make an inspirational movie: young American drops out of the fast-lane advertising world to teach disadvantaged Spanish kids so they can get a leg up in the stultified caste system of Spanish education. The kids are unruly, but endearing. The teacher? Earnest and driven; he is finally redeemed by his good works and forgets he was ever a cold, selfish purveyor of consumerism. His reward? That's obvious: the plucky, high-minded physical therapist! Now that's a movie.

—Why are you so cynical?

—Claudia, we'll talk about it some other time.

—You swear?

—I swear.

The tune playing through the place at that moment was Sinéad O'Connor's alluring *Nothing Compares To You*, that year's ubiquitous tune. I raised my glass to her.

—The song's about you, my steadfast, pure-hearted girl.

We hugged there in the middle of the café, oblivious to others. Then Sinéad O'Connor was followed by Annie Lennox and *Sweet Dreams*.

—This song is from 1984, the year I arrived in Spain. This is where I came into this movie.

—The movie has a sequel—she said. And she kissed me.

—You know, Claudia, I wonder what someone as well-intentioned as you is doing with me. And I think I know. I think Spanish women are attracted to men, not out of passion, but out of *com*passion.

—Not true.

And she kissed me again.

I bought some things to take back to my place: *manchego* cheese, smoked salmon and some crabmeat canapés. The night was moist and syrupy and, from the park, a breeze blew toward us, fluffy and green.

When we got to my place, I went straight to the kitchen to get plates and silverware.

—Kevin, you have one phone message—called out Claudia from the living room.

—Go ahead and play it.

And, in a second, even from way back in the kitchen, I heard the loud, sour voice and winced. It was Sloane Endicott. And she was drunk.

—Hey, you fucker! So you don't like American women, huh? You deserter, you ... ingrate! I was practically throwing myself at you today. Hell, I was throwing myself at you back in school! What is your problem, you ...?

I rushed to the answering machine and erased the message.

—I'm sorry, Claudia.

She looked up at me, pained and confused. Then she began to cry.

—What's wrong, Claudia? It's only a crazy girl from fifteen years ago that I met for a drink. It's meaningless.

—Not to her!—She blurted out between sobs.

I looked at the ceiling.

—I can't help that. But I never had a relationship with her.

—But what about the next one? And the one after that? I can't help thinking about you with other women. How am I going to keep them away from you? You've got looks, education, money and a sense of humor. And I? I'm this little, lower-middle-class *catalana* who doesn't drink, doesn't fly and is way too serious for this country.

—Claudia, please.

She pushed me away.

—You know, we women are different. We don't like a man because he's got the right look or the right job, but because he's got the right <u>flaws</u>; the ones we can <u>live</u> with! And, as it happens, I can live with <u>yours</u>! I can live with your selfishness, your opaqueness and your total allergy to showing emotion. I can!

She was sobbing openly now.

—I also know I'm not the most interesting woman you've known, nor the most gregarious, nor the most beautiful. But, damn it, I <u>love</u> you!

I took her in my arms. Her body heaved in spasms against mine.

—You're wrong about one thing—I said.

—W-what?—She had calmed down some.

—You <u>are</u> the most beautiful woman I've ever known.

She looked up at me, her wet blue eyes blinking.

—It's just that, right now, I have issues that I have to deal with alone: I have to find work and I have to find a way of staying in Spain legally.

She shuffled over to the refrigerator, opened it and took out a carrot.

Then she looked at me.

—Well, in the worst of the cases, the worst—she said, snapping off the end of the carrot with her teeth and sucking back a sniffle—I could always marry you.

And I let her do just that.

THE END

978-0-595-43351-3
0-595-43351-0

Author's note to the reader

Why do people leave their countries?
Yes, there's oppression, persecution and sheer desperate need. But how to explain the *American* expatriate? If he's not running from any of those things, what is he running *to*?

I believe America, despite the infinite bounty that is such a magnet to millions, leaves some of us aching, not with any urgent pain, but with a dull hollowness in parts that we seek to fill.

Yet, when we do spy the eventual new home, there is no epiphany. In fact, we often fight against it (as it fights against us). I know a New Yorker posted to Hong Kong who hated the place and its crowds so much that he walked in the middle of traffic to avoid the blank multitudes streaming toward him on the sidewalks. Twenty years later, this now-fluent Cantonese speaker says: "Hong Kong is like Manhattan, man. But with a lot more *juice*!"

Americans are also not necessarily tugged at by the high-minded ideals of a foreign culture. Sweden is an open, liberal country, virtually discrimination-free, that takes care of its people. But a longtime resident there, originally from Texas, tells me: "Darlin', nobody lands in Stockholm, falls to his knees and yells 'Hosanna!' It ain't that kinda deal."

I don't believe Americans respond to any grand social symphony in a foreign country, but, rather, to the euphonic hum of the everyday: the food markets, the way people drive, the radio programs, the cab drivers, the feel of the newspapers and the colors of the stamps. Maybe it's the way people wait in line at the bakery, the sirens of the police cars, or the way the women laugh. Sometimes it's the children with their grandparents in the evening on the square. Or simply the shapes of the trees, the look of the dogs, the smell of the barbershops. The taste of the rain.

I love Spanish rain.

It takes time to rub up against the rough spots of a country, if you're ever going to stay. Years, maybe. And, if you ever achieve any kind of fit, it means your own shape has changed, too.

It means the key has found its lock.

Printed in the United States
81569LV00003B/301-384